AF668120

# NEELADRI

## The Protector of the Mountains

HIMANSHU PANWAR

First Published in June 2025

ISBN: 978-93-342-4632-2

Cover Design: Himanshu

Typographic Design: Himani Goel

To My Parents,

Everything I have and everything I am, I owe it all to you.
Thank you for everything. God Bless.

To My Daughter, Anaya

Three years of magic, now walking into a world of even more. Bless you! Well-being and Joy

# Preface

Stories have always fascinated me, particularly those that intertwine the natural world with the mystical. Mountains, in their towering majesty, have a way of commanding both awe and fear. They remind us of our insignificance, of the raw power of nature, and yet they also cradle secrets that whisper through their valleys and echo against their peaks. For me, writing this story was about exploring the profound connection between humans and the places they inhabit, the legacy they leave behind, and the forces they often don't fully understand.

This story was born out of questions I've often pondered while wandering through the mountains myself: What drives people to settle in such harsh, unforgiving terrains? What keeps them rooted despite the challenges, and what compels them to eventually abandon these sacred lands? Is it the allure of progress or the whispers of something ancient—something they've tried to forget but cannot escape? These questions served as the foundation for this narrative.

The cursed land in this story isn't just a plot device. It's a metaphor for the delicate balance between humans and nature, tradition and change, belief and doubt. Growing up, I've always been drawn to tales of demigods and devils, stories of faith and fear, and the moral complexities they often embody. They reflect our inner struggles as much as our external ones. In crafting this story, I wanted to delve into the gray areas of human behavior—how fear can bind a community together but also tear it apart, and how belief can be both a guiding light and a shackle.

This book also reflects a deep respect for the traditions and beliefs of mountain communities. These are people who have carved lives out of the wilderness, guided by rituals and gods who are as much a part of their identity as the soil they till and the rivers they drink from. Yet, they too face the pressures of a changing world. Migration, commercialization, and urbanization threaten to erode not just their way of life but also their connection to their land and its spirits. Through this narrative, I wanted to shine a light on this struggle and invite readers to reflect on what we stand to lose when we sever those ties.

At its heart, this story is about the stories we tell ourselves—to make sense of the world, to find meaning in suffering, and to give shape to the invisible forces that govern our lives. It's about the intersection of myth and reality, where truths are cloaked in legends and faith becomes a compass in uncharted territory. I wanted to write a tale that feels timeless yet urgent, steeped in the mystery of the past but resonating with the challenges of the present.

Writing this story was as much an exploration for me as I hope reading it will be for you. It's a journey into the unknown, a descent into the depths of belief and the heights of doubt. It's about the power of fear to protect and destroy, the resilience of traditions, and the questions that refuse to be silenced.

I leave you with this: Do we shape the land we inhabit, or does it shape us? What happens when we forget the agreements forged with the past? And when the mountains speak, will we listen? Thank you for embarking on this journey with me. The answers may not all be here, but perhaps, that's the point. The story is not over. It's never over. After all, the mountains remember.

# Prologue

The mountains have always kept their secrets well. Beneath the towering peaks, wrapped in veils of mist and shadows, they stand as silent witnesses to centuries of human struggle, devotion, and folly. In their folds lie stories of gods and devils, whispered through generations yet never fully understood.

For centuries, Neeladri, the revered and feared demigod, has protected the villagers of their secluded region. His warnings, delivered with an authority none would question, have shaped the lives of those who dwell here.

For generations, the villagers lived by his decree: *Stay away from the cursed land.*

The villagers of Neeladri's domain knew this truth all too well. They had lived under the shadow of his blessings and his warnings. For them, the mountains were both home and enigma, a sanctuary and a challenge. Life here was a delicate balance between reverence and resilience, between fear and faith.

No one dared question why. The barren stretch of land was untouched, shunned as if by instinct. Children grew up fearing its edges, while elders spoke of misfortune befalling those who dared stray too close. It was an unspoken rule, an invisible barrier etched into the consciousness of the community.

But whispers of change began to stir.

When outsiders arrived, armed with ambition and disregard for ancient warnings, the villagers found themselves caught between reverence for the old ways and the lure of progress. Among these outsiders was Asuran, a man with wealth, power, and an unyielding disbelief in curses. To him, the cursed land was nothing but an untapped resource, its ominous history merely a tale spun by frightened minds.

Yet, some questions refused to stay buried.

Do curses hold power, or is fear the greatest force of all?

Why did their ancestors settle in these harsh mountains?

What price did they pay for survival?

And what did they awaken in their desperation?

Some questions refuse to be answered. Some truths are too dangerous to uncover.

The mountains are watching. Neeladri is waiting.

Will you listen to the warnings, or will curiosity lead you into the shadows?

# Chapters

# The Curse of Plain Terrain

In the stillness of the ancient forest, a temple stood quietly among the tall pine trees, their branches swaying gently in the cold breeze. A drizzle hung in the air, refreshing but not enough to get you wet. It felt like the rain was just a whisper, not meant to break the peace. The scent of pine mixed with the earthy smell of damp soil, filled the air with a calming fragrance. The trees surrounded the temple like silent guardians, their deep green leaves rustling in the breeze. Above, the sky was a soft gray, and the mountains in the distance stood tall and majestic, their peaks almost hidden by the mist. The land felt alive, breathing in harmony with nature.

Below the temple, nestled in the valley, was a small, peaceful village. A river flowed gently nearby, its soft murmur blending with the wind. The whole place felt timeless as if it had always been this way—quiet, untouched, and sacred.

But three hundred years ago, this land was not the village it is today. It was a vast, uncultivated wilderness. The hills were thick with wild forests, the river cutting its path through dense, uncharted woods. There were no homes, no fields, just the wild, waiting for someone to bring life to it. This land had always been full of potential, but it was empty, untouched by human hands. That all changed when people arrived, drawn by the whispers of a land that promised peace, prosperity, and a simple life.

These people were not running from poverty, but from the busy, chaotic cities that were growing beyond the mountains. They sought a life free from the noise and rush, a place where nature was their guide and the land was sacred. They came in small groups, families looking for something more—something they couldn't find in the busy streets of the cities. They didn't want to conquer the land; they wanted to live with it, in harmony with it. The forest, the river, the mountains—they wanted to be a part of it all.

The first years were difficult. The land was wild and stubborn. But little by little, they learned how to live with it. They built homes from the stone and wood of the mountains, careful not to disturb the land more than necessary. They grew crops, fed by the rich soil and nourished by the river that ran through the valley. Slowly, the village began to take shape, a peaceful settlement where the people lived in balance with nature. They didn't measure their wealth in gold or possessions but in peace and happiness.

Over time, as the village grew, the outside world began to call again. The cities, now full of opportunities and ambition, drew the younger generation away. It wasn't that they were poor—it was the desire for something more, a different kind of life. Every year, more young people left to chase those dreams, seeking careers and possibilities beyond the hills. But even though they left, they always came back—every year, for the annual Pooja ceremony, to remember the land, the village, and the sacred bond they shared.

As the years passed, the village grew and changed. People came, and some left, but the spirit of the village remained. The land, the river, and the mountains continued to nurture the people who called this place home, a home where they could live in peace, away from the rush of the world beyond. And no matter how much time passed or how far the young ones traveled, they always returned—to this land, to this village, to this sacred place that had been their home for generations.

Every year, the villagers celebrate the **'Annual Prayer Ritual'**, a grand ceremony in honor of the holiest demigod Neeladri, their protector and source of all prosperity. This was not just a ritual; it was a deep, spiritual connection to the divine. The entire village came together, their hearts filled with gratitude and reverence, as they offered their prayers to the mountain god.

As the sun dipped below the horizon, casting a golden glow over the land, the villagers gathered around the ancient temple in the heart of the village. The **idol of Neeladri**, carved from the stone of the mountain itself, stood tall at the center, bathed in the flickering light of a hundred candles. The idol's features were so lifelike that one could almost imagine it coming to life at any moment.

The villagers, young and old, sat in a circle around the temple, the air thick with a sense of divinity. Some had tears in their eyes, others sat in stunned silence, overwhelmed by the sacredness of the moment. Yet, among them stood **Kumarsen Rama,** a young man in his late twenties, with a troubled look on his face. His heart was at peace, yet a strange unease lingered in his mind. Something felt... different this year.

A soft voice broke the silence. **Ramesh**, a fellow villager, spoke quietly, his face drawn with concern. "The young ones are leaving, Kumarsen," he said. "Every year, more of them go to the cities. Not because we are poor, but because they are chasing after something more... opportunities, they say."
Kumarsen nodded, glancing at the other villagers. His brow furrowed in thought. "They say the cities are full of dreams. But we were happy here... weren't we?"

Another voice joined in, that of **Sulochana**, a middle-aged woman known for her wisdom. "It's not just our village," she said, her voice tinged with sadness. "It's every village in the hills. The young ones go looking for better living standards. They don't leave because they must, but because they desire more."

Ramesh, ever the optimist, offered a gentle smile. "But they always come back for the Pooja, don't they? No matter where they are, they make sure to come home for this."

Kumarsen's gaze drifted to the distant hills, the familiar faces of his fellow villagers filling him with a mixture of pride and sorrow. "I hope so," he said softly. "But what if they don't come back? What if we lose this connection with the land, with Neeladri?"

Sulochana placed a hand on his shoulder. "We can only do our part, Kumarsen. We must keep the flame of worship alive, pass it on to the younger generation."

The conversation turned to the changes sweeping through the village. The younger generation, once devoted to the traditions of the past, was now being drawn to the allure of the modern world, a world they thought would offer them more. The elders spoke of the fading tradition, of the risks they faced if they didn't continue to honor the divine forces that had always guided them.

One of the village's oldest and wisest men, **Chandran**, spoke slowly, his voice like gravel. "Neeladri never asks us for anything, Kumarsen. He gives us his blessings freely. But it is our duty to remember him, to worship him, to keep the tradition alive. This isn't just about the Pooja—it's about our connection to the earth, to the mountains, to him."

Kumarsen sighed deeply. "But what happens if the young ones forget? If they don't come back? What will become of us then?"

"There's still time," Sulochana replied, her tone filled with hope. "We must keep the flame burning. We must pass it on."

As the sun dipped below the mountains, the villagers gathered around the temple. The **idol of Neeladri** gleamed softly in the twilight, its stone features almost alive in the candlelight. At the front stood **Rayan**, the village priest, tall and calm, his eyes filled with a knowledge that seemed beyond his years. His presence radiated wisdom, and when he spoke, his voice carried the weight of a thousand stories.

The villagers placed their offerings—fruits, flowers, incense—at the base of the idol. They were silent, each lost in their own thoughts and prayers. Rayan raised his hands to the heavens, and as he began to chant, his voice seemed to resonate with the very air around them.

"O Neeladri, protector of this land, hear our prayer. May your blessings fill this village with peace and prosperity."
The chant was ancient, its rhythm as old as the mountains themselves. The air grew thick with the power of the words, and the ground beneath the villagers' feet seemed to hum with energy. The villagers closed their eyes, hands raised in prayer, their hearts filled with reverence.
In that moment, time seemed to stand still. The only sound was Rayan's voice, the soft rustle of leaves in the trees, and

the distant call of a bird. The air itself seemed to pause, waiting for something—something monumental—to happen.

**And then, it did.**

A sudden stillness filled the air, followed by a heavy tension that none of the villagers could explain. Rayan, standing at the altar, had stopped chanting. His eyes were closed, his face slack, as though he were listening to something beyond the realm of mortal understanding. A strange energy began to build, an unseen force that made the villagers uneasy.

Suddenly, a brilliant flash of light erupted from the idol of Neeladri. It was blinding, and the entire temple seemed to glow with a golden brilliance. The villagers gasped, instinctively taking a step back. The ground beneath them trembled, ever so slightly, and a strange hum filled the air, like the sound of a storm gathering far away.

The light pulsed and swirled, growing brighter with each passing second. The villagers shielded their eyes, stunned and uncertain of what they were witnessing. And then, just as quickly as it had come, the light faded, leaving behind an eerie silence.

When the villagers opened their eyes, what they saw was not the priest, Rayan, but something far more ancient. The figure that stood before them was **Neeladri**, the demigod, and he was no longer confined to his stone form.

Rayan's body remained the same, but his eyes—those eyes—glowed with an otherworldly light. His posture had changed. Where once he stood humbly as a priest, he now carried himself with the **grace of a god**. His shoulders were broad, his movements slow yet deliberate, as though he were both **part of the earth** and above it at the same time.

The villagers froze, unsure whether to kneel or run. But they couldn't tear their eyes away from the figure before them. Neeladri's presence was both terrifying and awe-inspiring, a force of nature that was as comforting as it was overwhelming.

Neeladri raised his hands, his voice filling the temple with a deep resonance. "**Rise, my people. I have come to meet you all.**" His voice carried the power of the mountains themselves, sending a ripple of fear and reverence through the villagers' hearts.

The demigod's gaze swept over the gathered villagers. His eyes were calm, yet something was unsettling about them—something that made them feel as though he could see straight through to their very souls. They bowed their heads instinctively, unable to move, as Neeladri began to walk among them.

“**Fear not, for I am here.**” His voice rang out, deep and commanding. “**You have honored me. Now, I bless every one of you.**”

One by one, the villagers fell to their knees, their hearts filled with awe and fear. Their offerings of water and flowers were presented to Neeladri, who accepted them with delicate hands. As he drank from each humble pot, the villagers watched in stunned silence.

The water shimmered as it touched his lips, glowing with a strange, ethereal light. When he finished, Neeladri threw the pot high into the air. The villagers gasped as it shattered, turning to fine dust that was absorbed into the earth itself.

With each offering, the tension in the air grew, and yet, the villagers’ fear began to dissipate, replaced by a profound sense of wonder. Neeladri was not just an idol—they could feel his presence, his power, walking among them.

When the last offering had been made, Neeladri turned toward the group, his voice carrying a weight beyond mortal comprehension. “*My thirst has been quenched. Thank you for Bhagirathi nectar, drawn with care and devotion. Each sip fills me with your faith and strengthens the bond between us."*

***

As the ceremony neared its conclusion, the sacred atmosphere lingered in the air, as if the village itself held its breath in anticipation. The villagers, a tapestry of hope and reverence, stood united under the twilight sky. The flames of the ceremonial torches flickered gently, casting dancing shadows across their faces. They knew the moment was near—the time when Neeladri, now manifesting through Rayan, would address them directly.

Neeladri, inhabiting the mortal form of their priest, stood tall and composed at the altar. The divine presence emanating from him was undeniable. His glowing eyes scanned the gathering, each villager feeling the weight of his gaze as if he could see into their very souls. Then, with a voice that was both human and celestial, he spoke.

"If any among you has a question or burden to share, speak now," Neeladri said.

His tone was calm, yet it carried a resonance that commanded attention, echoing in the stillness like a song from the mountains themselves.

The villagers exchanged uncertain glances, their hearts pounding. Few would dare to speak in such a sacred moment. Yet they knew this was their opportunity—a rare chance to converse with the divine.

After a moment's hesitation, **Kumarsen** stepped forward. He was younger than many of the elders but respected for his thoughtfulness and courage. His heart raced as he approached, and he bowed deeply before Deva Neeladri. When he rose, his voice was steady, though his nerves trembled beneath the surface.

"Great Neeladri," Kumarsen began, his words measured and filled with reverence. "We are grateful beyond words for your blessings. You have given us peace, happiness, and all that we could ever ask for. We live in abundance, and we know it is because of your grace. For this, we thank you."

Neeladri nodded, his glowing gaze softening ever so slightly. "Your gratitude honors me. Speak freely, Kumarsen."

Encouraged by the demigod's calm demeanor, Kumarsen continued. "There is something that troubles us, my lord. Not a complaint, for we have none. It is merely a question—a mystery that we, your humble people, cannot unravel."

Neeladri's expression remained unreadable, but the faint hum of energy around him seemed to shift. The villagers leaned in, their curiosity mirrored in their anxious silence.

"There is a piece of land," Kumarsen said, his voice growing firmer, "a thousand acres, not far from our village. It has been barren for as long as anyone can remember. No crops will grow there, no matter how hard we try. The soil refuses to yield. It is said to be cursed. Some even believe it is touched by black magic. Why is this land so? Why can't we make use of it? What is its purpose?"

The air grew heavy with tension. Even the faint rustling of the pine trees seemed to quiet, as though nature itself awaited the answer. The villagers' eyes shifted from Kumarsen to Neeladri, their faces a mixture of fear and hope.

Neeladri's luminous eyes darkened slightly, his celestial aura taking on a more somber tone. The air around him grew colder, and the villagers felt an unspoken weight pressing down on their hearts. When he finally spoke, his voice was calm, but it carried an edge that sent shivers down their spines.

"**This land,**" Neeladri began, his tone grave, "is not for you. It is disputed ground, bound by forces older and more powerful than any of you can comprehend. I have given you all that you need—happiness, prosperity, and peace. Why do you seek more?"

The question hung in the air, and Kumarsen felt his chest tighten. He bowed his head in deference but dared to speak again. "We do not seek out of greed, my lord," he said softly. "We only wish to understand. This land lies so close to our homes, yet it is lifeless. Is there truly no way to bring it to life? To make it part of the bounty you have given us?"

Neeladri's gaze softened briefly, but his reply remained resolute. "This land is dangerous," he said, his voice now laced with warning. "It holds a power that must remain undisturbed. To awaken it would be to invite ruin. It is best forgotten. You and your fellow villagers must stay away from it. There is nothing there for you—only destruction."

The villagers shifted uneasily, their initial curiosity giving way to fear. Kumarsen's heart raced as he processed the weight of Neeladri's words. He glanced back at the crowd, seeing their unease reflected in their faces. This wasn't the answer they had hoped for, but it was one they couldn't ignore.

"But, Great Neeladri," Kumarsen pressed, his voice barely above a whisper, "is there truly no way? Could we not purify the land? Lift the curse? Surely, with your divine power…"

**Neeladri raised a hand, silencing him.** The gesture was not harsh, but it carried an undeniable finality. His eyes, glowing with an intensity that seemed to pierce through Kumarsen's very being, left no room for argument.

"**This land is cursed**," Neeladri said, his words sharp and deliberate. "And it is cursed for a reason. It holds a power that, if awakened, will bring devastation upon all you hold dear. It is not for you to meddle with."

A deep silence settled over the crowd. The villagers exchanged nervous glances, their hopes of reclaiming the land now eclipsed by the weight of Neeladri's warning.

Kumarsen bowed his head, his frustration mingling with a newfound sense of foreboding.

Neeladri's gaze swept over the villagers once more, his expression softening as he addressed them. "Be content with what you have," he said, his tone now gentler. "What I have given you is enough. You are blessed beyond measure. Do not let your hearts be burdened by what you cannot change."

The demigod turned back toward the altar, his presence still commanding but no longer as intense. The villagers bowed deeply, their hearts heavy with the weight of his words. They knew better than to question further. The cursed land would remain an unanswered mystery, a shadow lingering on the edge of their otherwise prosperous lives.

As the crowd dispersed, murmurs of both awe and unease rippled through the village. Some spoke of the wisdom in Neeladri's words, while others couldn't shake the feeling that the barren land held secrets far more dangerous than they had imagined. Kumarsen, walking silently among his fellow villagers, felt a growing determination in his heart. He knew he should heed Neeladri's warning, but the mystery of the cursed land had rooted itself in his mind.

For now, the demigod's word was final. But Kumarsen couldn't help but wonder if the truth about the land would remain buried forever—or if fate would one day force it into the light.

## The Outsiders' Arrival

The crisp morning air carried the soft rustle of pine needles as Kumarsen stood near the village temple, watching the mist swirl between the trees. The quiet calm was interrupted by the confident crunch of boots on the gravel path. Asuran Das, a businessman from the plains, approached with an air of determination.

"Kumarsen," Asuran began, his voice smooth but firm, "did you ask the demigod about the land?"

Kumarsen turned to face him, his sharp eyes locking onto Asuran's. "I did. Neeladri was clear. The land is cursed, and we are to leave it alone."

Asuran scoffed, shaking his head. "Cursed? Come now, Kumarsen, do you truly believe that? Curses and myths are for stories, not for real life. We live in a modern world."

Kumarsen crossed his arms, his stance unwavering. "This village has thrived because we respect the land, the spirits, and the demigod. If Neeladri warns us to stay away, we do so. It's not for you to question."

Asuran took a step closer, lowering his voice. "Do you know how rare such land is? Flat, fertile, a thousand acres of plain terrain in the middle of hills and mountains? In this entire region, it's almost impossible to find. Peaks, valleys, snow-covered ridges—those we expect. But flat land like that? It's a gift."

"It's unnatural," Kumarsen countered, his voice steady. "There's a reason that land is vacant, untouched, and feared. Land like that, sitting barren for generations, doesn't happen without a cause. It's not a gift, Asuran. It's a warning."

Asuran's lips curled into a smile, but it didn't reach his eyes. "Warnings, curses… you hill folk are good at spinning tales. But this is just nature. Uncommon, yes, but not impossible. Land like this exists in the world—it's rare, but not cursed. And it's wasted. What's the point of letting it sit idle when it could transform this village?"

"Transform?" Kumarsen raised an eyebrow. "What you call transformation, I call greed. You want to fill that land with apartments, don't you? Build your 2,500 luxury homes and sell the hills to outsiders who care nothing for this place."

"Why not?" Asuran shot back, his tone hardening. "Why shouldn't this village have better roads, hospitals, schools? Tourists would flood in. The economy would boom. Your children could have a future beyond farming and storytelling. Isn't that worth it?"

"And what if the curse is real?" Kumarsen's voice cut through the morning air like a blade. "What if your machines disturb something that shouldn't be touched? What if your grand plans bring destruction, not prosperity?"

Asuran laughed, shaking his head. "You give too much power to myths. What can Neeladri do in this? A demigod cannot stop progress, Kumarsen. All you and the landowners need to do is sign a piece of paper. After that, it's out of your hands."

Kumarsen's eyes burned with quiet defiance. "You think this is just about signatures? About papers and laws? This land isn't like the plains you come from, Asuran. It's alive. The mountains, the rivers, the forests—they have their own will, their own spirit. Neeladri isn't just a protector of our faith; he's a protector of the balance. And you're arrogant enough to challenge that?"

Asuran leaned in, his voice low and threatening. "Listen, Kumarsen. I've promised Mr. Logan that this land will be developed. I've hired experts—scientists, spiritual advisors, even curse-breakers. They all say the same thing: there's nothing to fear. This is just a piece of land, waiting to be used. It's time for you and your villagers to move forward, not cling to the past."

Kumarsen's voice remained calm but firm. "Move forward into what? Concrete towers and broken promises? Do you think your luxury apartments will bring happiness here? You'll destroy what makes this village special—its peace, its unity, its connection to the land. You don't understand what you're tampering with."

Asuran's patience was wearing thin. "What I understand is opportunity. That land is a gold mine, Kumarsen. And if you don't see it, you're a fool. Sign the papers, and your village will reap the rewards. Refuse, and you'll be left behind. This isn't a threat—it's reality."

"You're wrong," Kumarsen said, his voice unwavering. "Reality is what we live every day, not the dream you're trying to sell. We have enough here—enough to live, enough to thrive. We don't need your apartments or your false promises."

Asuran's expression darkened, his polished veneer cracking. "Mark my words, Kumarsen. That land will be mine, with or without your cooperation. You can stand in my way if you want, but you'll only make things harder for yourself and your people."

Kumarsen stepped forward, his presence towering despite the difference in their worlds. "You underestimate this village, Asuran. We've faced storms, droughts, and hardships far worse than you. We stand together, and we stand with Neeladri. You can try to force your will on this land, but you'll find it fights back. And so will we."

For a moment, the two men stood in tense silence, the weight of their confrontation hanging in the air. Finally, Asuran turned on his heel, his boots crunching against the gravel as he walked away.

Kumarsen watched him go, his heart heavy but his resolve stronger than ever. He knew Asuran wouldn't give up easily, but neither would the village. The battle for the cursed land was far from over, but Kumarsen had faith in the strength of his people and the power of Neeladri's protection.

As the wind whispered through the trees, carrying the faint scent of pine and earth, Kumarsen turned back toward the village. The path ahead would be difficult, but he was ready to face whatever came next.

***

The room smelled of cigar smoke, mingling with the scent of old wood and leather. Asuran sat behind his massive desk, his fingers drumming restlessly against the polished surface. Outside, the storm gathered strength, the rumble of thunder a soft growl in the distance. **Vettison**, his trusted lawyer cum goon, stood leaning casually against the wall, arms crossed, but his eyes sharp and calculating.

Asuran leaned forward, his gaze intense. "Vettison, this village is holding onto that land like it's some sort of treasure. But it's not. It's a barren wasteland. Yet, they refuse to see it. That land could be worth a fortune, and they're sticking to their superstitions."

Vettison shrugged, not bothered by Asuran's frustration. "It's not just superstitions, Asuran. To them, Neeladri's word is law. If he says the land is cursed, they believe it without question."

Asuran scoffed, the edges of his mouth curling in disdain. "Neeladri. The so-called protector of these hills. It's ridiculous. If I can't break through this, Mr. Logan will pull out of the deal. That land is perfect for his project—2,500 luxury apartments, all with hill views. Do you have any idea what that's worth? Millions, maybe more."

Vettison nodded, his mind already working. "Millions, yes. But the villagers? They don't think in dollars. They think in faith and fear. And right now, they're paralyzed by both."

Asuran's jaw tightened. "Then we use that fear to our advantage. How do we break them, Vettison? How do we make them see that this so-called curse is nothing but a fairytale?"

Vettison straightened, meeting Asuran's gaze with a calm determination. "You've got two options. Either we prove the curse is just a myth, or we show them how much they're losing by holding on to it."

Asuran exhaled sharply. "Proving it's fake—that's your job, then. But how do we show them they're throwing away a fortune by clinging to these old stories?"

**Vettison** paused for a moment, thinking, his eyes flicking toward the window, where the storm clouds were darkening. "First, we need to figure out what the curse is. Right now, it's all vague talk—no crops, bad luck, some kind of evil spirit. We need details. What's behind this curse? Once we know that, we can use it to undermine the whole thing."

Asuran leaned back in his chair, steepling his fingers. "I like that. Expose the curse for the nonsense it is. But what about the second option you mentioned? The one about their future?"

Vettison's eyes gleamed with a sharp, calculating light. "You have to appeal to their ambitions. Show them what that land could do for their futures. Hotels, restaurants, tourist businesses. That land could make them rich. Their young men and women wouldn't have to move to the cities anymore. They could come back, start businesses here, and build something real. It's their chance to stop being poor forever."

Asuran's lips curled into a slow smile, but there was no warmth in it. "And you think they'll listen? You think they'll buy that? They've been living in this village for generations, clinging to their way of life. This isn't going to be easy."

Vettison nodded thoughtfully. "Not everyone will buy it. But some of them will. If we can make them see the bigger picture, they'll realize that the land is an opportunity, not a curse. And once a few of them are on board, the rest will follow. It's just a matter of starting with the right people."

Asuran considered this for a moment, the wheels in his mind turning quickly. "And what if they don't listen? What if they refuse to sign the papers? What do we do then?"

Vettison's voice dropped lower, a hint of something darker creeping into his tone. "That's where we need to get creative. We don't just show them the benefits—we make them feel the consequences. If they won't act in their best interests, we'll make them see how their refusal hurts not just them, but their children, their families, their entire future."

Asuran raised an eyebrow, intrigued by the idea. "Go on."

Vettison's smile was cold, his voice now smooth and calculated. "You know as well as I do that the young people in the village are already leaving. They're going to the cities for work, for a better life. The older generation doesn't see it, but the village is dying. If they hold onto this land and refuse to modernize, they'll have no one left in a generation. They'll fade away into nothing. You tell them that. Tell them the truth: if they don't act now, their children will never come back. They'll be forgotten. But if they agree to sell, if they see the future of the land, their children will return. They'll have businesses, homes, families. A legacy."

Asuran's eyes glittered with anticipation. "I see. Emotional manipulation. It's dirty, but effective. I like it. And if they still don't agree?"

Vettison's smile turned grim. "Then we push them harder. We remind them what's at stake. Their children's futures. Their survival as a community. And if they still refuse, we make them understand that the world won't wait for them.

People will leave, and they'll have no one to blame but themselves."

Asuran stood up, pacing in the dim light. "I'll tell them the truth then, Vettison. This is their chance to save the village. This land is their way out of poverty. Their only way. If they don't take it, they'll have no one but themselves to blame."

Vettison nodded, his tone now firm. "Exactly. And if they still don't listen? Then we make sure they understand what happens when you stand in the way of progress."

Asuran stopped pacing and turned to face his lawyer. "We'll need to be careful. The villagers are proud, stubborn people. But this is too good of an opportunity to pass up. We'll break their resolve. And once they see the light, we'll take that land, and we'll build the future they've been too afraid to see."

Vettison smiled, the satisfaction in his expression clear. "We'll make them see it, Asuran. One way or another."

Asuran's smile was cold, a promise of inevitable success. **"Let's get started then."**

Vettison gave a sharp nod, his face unreadable, but his mind already racing with the next steps. Asuran had always been a man of action, but now, with the stakes higher than ever, Vettison knew they had to be precise, calculated, and ruthless. It was time to put their plan into motion.

Outside the room the wind howled like it might be the beginning of a storm in the sky. Inside, the tension was tangible. Asuran's impatience crackled in the dim light of his office, the flicker of a candle casting long shadows on the walls.

"We start by gathering information," Vettison said, his voice low and deliberate. "We need to know everything about that land—the history, the people, and most importantly, the Curse. If we can understand what holds them back, we can counter it."

Asuran leaned forward, his eyes narrowing. "And how do we get them to talk? How do we get inside their heads?"

Vettison curved his lips to give a cold smile, his hands steepling in front of him. "There are ways. You know that. First, we'll need to send someone into the village—a trusted ally. Someone they won't suspect. We need to speak to the elders, the ones who know the old stories. They're the ones who hold the key to the curse."

Now, Asuran's lips curled into a smile, but it wasn't one of warmth. " You believe the elders will spill their secrets?

Vettison's eyes gleamed. "Not immediately. But there are ways to coax the truth out. We'll approach them gently at first—make them feel comfortable. Then, we press a little harder and use their superstitions to our advantage. People like them are often more willing to share when they feel safe. Once we have the curse in detail, we can start to dismantle it."

Asuran stood up and paced the room, his mind turning the idea over. "And once we have the curse… what then?"

Vettison's voice was calm, almost reassuring. "Once we have it, we'll expose it. We'll show the villagers that the curse is nothing more than an old wives' tale. Something that's been keeping them chained to the past for generations. We'll make them see that the only thing truly holding them back is their refusal to let go."

Asuran stopped pacing, turning to Vettison with a sharp look. "But what if they still refuse, and refuse to sign those papers?"

Vettison's grin stretched further, a wicked gleam flickering in his eyes. "If they refuse, we apply more pressure. We show them the reality they're avoiding. We remind them what's at stake. Their children are already leaving, heading for the cities. They're abandoning the village for the very reasons we've discussed—the lack of opportunity. If they don't act now, they risk losing the last generation that still believes in this place."

Asuran's expression darkened. "You think they'll listen to that?

Vettison's eyes never wavered. "They'll have no choice. When faced with the truth, most people will bend. And if they still refuse, we'll use other means. There are ways to… persuade them."

Asuran's lips tightened in a thin smile. **"I trust you, Vettison. You know how to get results. Do it."**

Vettison stood up, straightening his jacket. "We'll need to move quickly. The longer we wait, the more time they have to grow suspicious. I'll send someone to the village tomorrow. Someone who knows how to approach the elders without drawing attention."

Asuran gave a sharp nod. "Good. And once we've gathered the information?"

Vettison's smile was slow and deliberate. "Once we have the curse, we'll have everything we need to break their resolve. We'll make them understand what they're throwing away. And once they sign those papers, we can begin our project."

The storm raged outside, its fury growing, but inside, the two men were calm. They were on the verge of something monumental, and nothing, no matter how difficult, would stand in their way.

As Vettison turned to leave, Asuran called out, his voice low but filled with intent. "And Vettison… no mistakes. If this fails, we don't just lose the land. We lose everything."

Vettison nodded, his expression steady. "There won't be any failures. I'll make sure of it."

# The Many Faces of the Curse

The next morning, the storm had subsided, leaving the village in an eerie quiet. The sky was overcast, casting a dull gray light over the hills. Vettison's trusted ally, a man named **Taran**, was already on his way to the village. Taran had lived in the hills once, many years ago, before moving to the city. He knew the people, and the customs, and most importantly, he understood the subtle ways to get what was needed without raising suspicion.

**Taran**'s mission was clear: speak to the elders, gain their trust, and learn everything about the curse on the land. He would approach them as a humble man, interested in hearing their stories and offering his help. But his true goal was to get the details of the curse, so that Vettison and Asuran could use it to dismantle the villagers' fears.

Taran walked up the winding path to the village, his mind sharp, focused on the task ahead. He had no illusions about the challenge before him. These people were stubborn, proud, and deeply rooted in their beliefs. But he had been trained to handle situations like this. He would use their own traditions, their own fears, against them.

As he reached the village, the familiar sight of the small stone houses and the narrow cobbled streets greeted him. He noticed the quietness, the absence of the usual bustle. The villagers were working, but there was a noticeable tension in the air. It was as if something had been disturbed, something important.

Taran made his way to the village square, where the elders usually gathered. He found them sitting in the shade of a large pine tree, their faces weathered with age but still sharp with the wisdom of years.

He bowed respectfully as he approached, his voice steady and calm. "Good day, baba. I hope I'm not interrupting. I've come to hear the stories of the land, to learn of its past."

The eldest elder, a woman named **Gaura**, looked him up and down, her eyes narrowing slightly. "What do you want with our stories, young man? The land has been cursed for generations. There is nothing to be gained from talking about it."

Taran smiled softly, a look of genuine curiosity on his face. "I've heard the stories, yes. But I'm interested in understanding. I want to know more about this curse. Perhaps there's something we can do to break it, to make the land fertile again. I'm willing to help in any way I can."

The elders exchanged glances, hesitant but intrigued. They were used to outsiders coming with promises of help, only to leave when their needs were met. But there was something different about Taran. His sincerity, the way he carried himself—it was enough to earn their attention.

**Gaura** sighed and motioned for him to sit. "Very well. But know this—there are things about this land that no outsider can understand. It is cursed, and there is no escaping it. It has taken many lives, and it will take more if we are not careful."

Taran leaned forward, listening intently. "Tell me what you know, Gaura. I am not here to challenge your beliefs, but to understand. Maybe, together, we can find a solution."

The elder hesitated for a moment, then began to speak, her voice low but steady, as if recounting a long-held secret. "It is said that long ago, the land was peaceful, fertile. But a terrible thing happened. A man, greedy for power, came to these hills. He wanted the land for himself, and in his desire, he angered the gods. The curse was born from that anger. The land became barren. The crops died. And now, nothing grows there."

Taran listened carefully, absorbing every word. He knew this was only the beginning. The story was incomplete, but it was a start.

"Who was this man?" he asked, his voice gentle. "And how did he anger the gods?"

Gaura's eyes grew darker. "The man's name was not spoken after that day. He was forgotten, as all who anger the gods should be. But his greed remains in the land, feeding the curse."

Taran smiled inwardly, knowing he had what he needed. He stood up slowly, his mind already turning. "Thank you, Gaura. I will speak to you again. Perhaps there is a way to break this curse after all."

As he walked away, his mind raced with possibilities. The curse was tied to greed, to a man who had long been forgotten. That was the key. Now, he just needed to find a way to use it—use the curse itself to break the villagers' resolve. They would have no choice but to sign the papers, once they understood that the past held no power over their future.

Vettison and Asuran were waiting, and Taran knew his next move would be crucial. The land, the curse, and the villagers' future—it was all about to change.

***

The following day, Taran walked through the village with a quiet determination, the weight of his mission pressing heavily on his shoulders. He had spoken with the elders, but their story was just the beginning. There were more people to speak with—more stories to uncover. The villagers were tight-lipped, but everyone had something to say. And he needed to hear it all.

He started with a middle-aged man, who sat outside his small stone house, idly tending to his garden. His hands were calloused from years of hard work, his face marked with the lines of both age and hard work.

Taran approached him respectfully, smiling as he took a seat nearby. "Good day, Sir. I've come to learn more about the land—the one near the edge of the village. I'm told it's cursed. Can you tell me about it?"

---

*The man paused in his work, wiping his hands on his trousers. He looked at Taran, his expression unreadable. "Cursed? You believe in curses, do you?" He gave a rough chuckle, but it quickly faded into a serious tone. "I'll tell you what I know. It was many years ago, that a young man came to the village. He was looking for land to settle on, land that would feed his family, and grow his crops. He was a stranger, but he had a good heart, and the village welcomed him. But greed... greed is what killed him. He struck a deal with the wrong people, and they turned on him. That's when the curse started. It was his actions that doomed the land—his greed, his desire for more. The gods don't look kindly on that."*

---

Taran nodded slowly, taking in the story, but something felt off. "And the curse? What exactly happened to the land?"

The man sighed, his eyes turning to the distant horizon. "Nothing grows. Nothing ever will again. The soil's been poisoned by that man's sins. It's like the land itself is angry. No one can touch it, not even the bravest of souls."

With that, he went back to his work, leaving Taran with more questions than answers. He thanked the man and moved on, his mind already processing the new information. The curse seemed tied to a man's actions, but the details were still vague. It wasn't the only story he would hear.

Next, Taran approached an older woman who had lived in the village her whole life. Her white hair framed a face filled with wisdom, though her eyes held a shadow of sadness. She sat by the fire outside her home, stirring a pot of soup.

"Good afternoon, I'm trying to understand more about the land, the cursed one. What do you know of it?" Taran asked gently, his voice low and respectful.

---

*She looked at him for a long moment, as if measuring his intentions. Finally, she spoke, her voice carrying the weight of years. "Ah, the cursed land. It's a story we don't tell often, but you've come to the right person." She paused and took a deep breath. "It wasn't always cursed. It was a beautiful piece of land, full of promise. But a long time ago, a family of travellers arrived—strangers from far away. They were welcomed, and given shelter by the village. But they had their own plans. They weren't here to settle, no. They were here to steal. They practiced dark magic, you see, and they used the land for their rituals. They desecrated the soil, took what wasn't theirs, and when they left, they left the land marked. It became barren, poisoned by their wickedness. The land was never the same after that. The gods saw what they did, and they cursed the land in return."*

---

Taran's brow furrowed. This version of the story seemed to differ from the last. "So, you're saying it wasn't the greed of one man, but a family of strangers who cursed it?"

Her face tightened. "A family, yes. And their dark ways. They thought they could control the land, and use its power for themselves. But they didn't know the power they were tampering with. The curse was their punishment. And we've all paid for it ever since."

Taran's mind raced. He thanked old woman and left her home, his thoughts tangled in confusion. Two different stories, each with its version of events, but both point to a deep-rooted malevolence tied to the land. Who was right? Or were they all wrong?

Taran's last stop was the village's blacksmith, an imposing man named **Kaalan**. His muscles were like steel, his hands marked by years of shaping metal, and his reputation for honesty and bluntness was well-known.

"**Kaalan**, I've heard tales about the cursed land near the village," Taran began, his voice steady. "I'd like to hear your version of the story. What do you know about it?"

---

*Kaalan looked up from his anvil, wiping the sweat from his brow. He leaned on the forge and looked Taran in the eye. "You've heard the rumors, I assume. People around here like to tell tales. But I know the truth. The curse wasn't brought by a person. No, it wasn't human greed or dark magic. It was the land itself. The gods tested the people here long ago. They wanted to see if we could live in peace with nature if we could balance our needs with the land's gifts. But some didn't care for that balance. Some took too much, and the gods punished them. The land turned against us. It was the gods' doing, not man's. And we've paid for it ever since."*

---

Taran's jaw tightened. A third version of the story, and yet none of them felt conclusive. Each story had its version of the truth, but none seemed to tell the full picture. What was he missing? Why were these people so divided over something so fundamental?

"I see," Taran said, forcing a polite smile. "Thank you, Kaalan."

The blacksmith gave a curt nod and returned to his work. Taran stood there for a moment, absorbing the weight of what he'd just learned. Each version of the curse was different, but there was one thread that ran through them all: fear. Fear of the land, fear of the unknown, fear of something beyond their control.

Taran returned to the inn where he was staying, sitting alone in his room, the stories swirling in his mind. None of them made sense together. The curse couldn't be explained by just one version. It wasn't just a story—it was a puzzle, and he needed to find the missing pieces.

He thought back to the elders and their words. They had told him little, only spoken in vague terms, but their fear had been real. And it was that fear that kept the village bound to the curse. But if they were all telling different stories, what did it mean? **Could the curse be real at all?**

Taran knew what he had to do next. He would have to dig deeper. He would need to confront the villagers with their fears and test their resolve. The curse had to have a source, and he would find it.

But he would need help. He would need someone who could look beyond the fear and get to the heart of the truth. **And there was only one person who could help him do that.**

**He was "Kumarsen Rama".**

The morning sunlight filtered through the tall windows of Asuran's office, casting long, slanted shadows on the polished wooden floor. Asuran sat at the head of the table, his fingers drumming on the armrest of his chair, a mix of impatience and curiosity on his face. Vettison stood by the window, arms crossed, staring out at the sprawling hills, as if trying to read the land itself.

The door creaked open, and Taran stepped inside. His face was a blend of exhaustion and determination, the kind of expression that promised revelations but carried their weight.

Asuran straightened, his voice sharp and direct. "Well, Taran? What did you find out?"

Taran shut the door behind him and took a seat across from Asuran. He placed his notebook on the table but didn't open it. "I spoke to the villagers. Three of them. But I'm afraid the answers aren't as straightforward as we hoped."

Asuran leaned forward, his eyes narrowing. "What does that mean?"

Taran sighed, running a hand through his hair. "It means that every person I talked to gave me a different version of the curse. Not just slightly different—completely different. It's like they're all carrying pieces of a puzzle, but none of them have the full picture."

Vettison turned from the window, his interest piqued. "Different how? Give us the details."

Taran met his gaze and began recounting the stories. "The first person I spoke to claimed the curse began because of a man's greed. He came to the village long ago, looking for land and prosperity, but his hunger for more led to betrayal and, eventually, a divine punishment. The land turned barren as a result of his sins."

Asuran scoffed, waving a dismissive hand. "A morality tale. Typical village nonsense. What else?"

"The second story," Taran continued, "was about a family of travelers. They supposedly performed dark rituals on the land, desecrating it. Their actions angered the gods, and the land was cursed as a result. The villager described it as a place tainted by something unholy, something no human should disturb."

Vettison frowned, his fingers tapping on the windowsill. "Dark magic? That's a convenient excuse for things people don't understand. And the third story?"

Taran hesitated, his voice lowering. "The third story was different. The villager claimed that the curse wasn't caused by man at all. They said it was the gods themselves testing the people—punishing them for taking too much from the land without giving back. According to this version, the land wasn't just cursed—it was a divine reminder of the balance they broke."

Silence hung in the room, heavy and contemplative.

Asuran broke it with a cold chuckle. "So, let me get this straight. One story blames greed, another blames magic, and the third blames the gods. Do any of these villagers actually know what they're talking about, or are they just spinning tales to keep us away?"

Taran shook his head. "That's exactly the problem. None of them know the truth. They've been repeating these stories for generations, but there's no consistency. It's all folklore, passed down and twisted over time. And that's why the curse has such a grip on them—because no one knows the real story."

Vettison stepped closer to the table, his face thoughtful. "If the stories are all different, it means one of two things: either the curse is fabricated, or there's something deeper that no one remembers. Either way, we need facts, not tales."

Asuran's eyes narrowed, his voice taking on a dangerous edge. "If the villagers don't know the truth, then their fear is baseless. That land isn't cursed—it's just misunderstood.

And misunderstanding can be fixed. But how do we get to the bottom of this? How do we find the truth?"

Taran leaned forward, his voice steady. "We need to go beyond the stories. Someone in this region—an elder, a historian, anyone—must have more concrete knowledge. Old records, forgotten texts, maybe even rituals that explain what really happened. If we can uncover the truth, we can dismantle the villagers' fear and prove that the land isn't cursed."

Vettison nodded, his expression resolute. "You're right. The stories are only part of the picture. We need evidence—something irrefutable."

Asuran's lips curled into a sly smile. "And once we have it, we'll use it to turn the villagers in our favor. They're clinging to their stories because that's all they have. If we give them the truth, they'll have no choice but to listen. This so-called curse will be nothing more than a footnote in their history."

Taran hesitated for a moment, then spoke carefully. "But there's one more thing. Even if we find the truth, we have to be prepared for the possibility that the curse is real. That it's not just a story."

Asuran's smile vanished, replaced by a cold, calculating glare. "Curses aren't real, Taran. They're tools of control—nothing more. We'll uncover the truth, and we'll break the villagers' grip on that land. But if you're afraid of fairy tales, maybe you're not the man for this job."

Taran's jaw tightened, but he didn't back down. "I'm not afraid, Asuran. I just think we need to be cautious. If there's even a chance that something supernatural is at play, we need to be ready for it."

Vettison stepped in, his voice calm but firm. "Let's not dismiss anything yet. We'll proceed carefully. First, we gather the facts. Then we act."

Asuran nodded reluctantly, his ambition still burning in his eyes. "Fine. Let's get to work. Taran, I want you to dig deeper. Find anyone who might have the answers we need. Vettison and I will handle the villagers in the meantime. The sooner we uncover the truth, the sooner we claim that land."

Taran rose from his seat, his resolve solidifying. "I'll start immediately. But remember—this isn't just about the land. It's about the people, their beliefs, and their history. If we're not careful, we could destroy more than just a story."

Asuran's eyes flashed with something unreadable, but he said nothing. Taran left the room, the weight of the task ahead pressing down on him. As he stepped out into the sunlight, he couldn't shake the feeling that the truth he sought might not be what anyone expected—or wanted to hear.

***

The morning air in the village was cool and crisp, carrying the faint aroma of pine trees and the distant hum of a mountain stream. Taran walked purposefully through the narrow lanes, his eyes scanning the quaint houses and the occasional curious villager who passed by. He spotted Kumarsen sitting outside his modest home, sipping tea from a clay cup, his expression calm yet focused.

Taran adjusted the strap of his satchel, taking a deep breath before approaching. "Excuse me, sir," he began, his voice warm and friendly. "I hope I'm not disturbing you."

Kumarsen looked up, his sharp eyes immediately assessing Taran. "Not at all. What brings you to our village?"

Taran smiled, his tone casual. "I'm a tourist, traveling through the hills. I've heard a lot about the beauty of this place and its rich history. But…" He hesitated, lowering his voice as if sharing a secret. "I also heard about a cursed land nearby. It piqued my curiosity. I couldn't help but wonder—what's the story behind it?"

Kumarsen's expression shifted subtly, a flicker of surprise crossing his face. "The cursed land?" he repeated, his voice guarded.

Taran nodded earnestly. "Yes. I'm also a writer, you see. I run a blog about hidden stories and mysterious places. When I heard about your village and the curse, I thought it would make for a fascinating piece. Of course, I don't mean to pry or disrespect your traditions. I'm just curious, that's all."

Kumarsen studied him for a long moment, then gestured to the empty stool beside him. "Curiosity can be dangerous, young man, but it can also lead to understanding. Sit. We'll talk."

Taran took the seat gratefully, his heart racing slightly. Kumarsen called into the house, and moments later, a young girl emerged with a tray of tea and biscuits.

After a sip of the steaming tea, Kumarsen leaned back in his chair, his gaze drifting to the distant mountains. "You're not the first outsider to ask about that land," he began, his voice low and reflective. "But I'll tell you what I know, or rather, what I don't know. Because that's the truth—nobody really knows."

Taran leaned in, his pen poised over his notebook. "What do you mean?"

Kumarsen smiled faintly. "The stories about the curse are as old as the village itself. Three hundred years ago, this place was nothing but wilderness. Our ancestors settled here, carving a life out of these mountains. But even then, that land was untouched. It's a flat plain—rare in these hills—but nothing ever grew there. People avoided it instinctively, as if they could sense something was wrong."

"What kind of stories have been told?" Taran pressed gently.

Kumarsen chuckled, shaking his head. "Too many to count. Some say the land was a battleground where ancient warriors shed their blood, and the earth refused to heal.

Others claim a family of sorcerers cursed it with dark magic to protect their treasures, and when they died, the curse remained. There's even a tale about the gods themselves marking it as sacred, forbidding mortals from disturbing it."

"And what do you believe?" Taran asked, his voice soft.

Kumarsen's smile faded. "I believe in Deva Neeladri. For three centuries, he has been our protector, our guide. When disasters strike, when crops fail, when sickness comes, we turn to him, and he never fails us. He is the reason this village has thrived for so long. And if Neeladri says to stay away from that land, we obey. No questions, no doubts."

Taran nodded, his brow furrowed. "But how does Neeladri communicate this? Do you see him? Hear him?"

Kumarsen hesitated, as if weighing his words. "Every year, during the grand festival, Neeladri chooses a vessel—a villager through whom he speaks. His words are sacred, his instructions absolute. Decades ago, someone asked about the land during the ceremony. Neeladri warned us never to touch it, never to disturb it. Since then, no one has dared bring it up again."

Taran's curiosity burned brighter. "Do you think it's possible to ask him again? Maybe just for clarification?"

Kumarsen shook his head firmly. "No. Neeladri's patience is not to be tested. His warning was clear, and to question him further would be seen as defiance. The villagers wouldn't stand for it, and neither would he."

Taran leaned back, processing this. "So, you're saying that if anyone wants to truly understand the curse, they'd have to hear it directly from Neeladri himself?"

Kumarsen nodded gravely. "Yes. But understand this—Neeladri doesn't owe explanations to anyone. Not to us, not to outsiders. If you approach him with questions, you risk not only angering him but also losing the trust of the villagers. To them, Neeladri's word is final. It's not just about the land—it's about their faith, their way of life. Do you really want to challenge that?"

Taran met Kumarsen's gaze, feeling the weight of his words. "I don't want to challenge anyone or anything," he said quietly. "I just want to understand. To uncover the truth, whatever it may be."

Kumarsen studied him for a moment, then sighed. "If that's your path, you'll have to walk it carefully. But I'll tell you this—truth is a double-edged sword. Sometimes, it can bring clarity and closure. Other times, it can destroy everything it touches. Be sure you're ready for whatever you find."

Taran nodded, his resolve hardening. "Thank you, Kumarsen. I'll keep that in mind."

As the two men sat in silence, the faint sound of a temple bell echoed through the village, a reminder of the presence that loomed over them all. For Taran, it was a sound both haunting and inviting—a call to uncover the mysteries hidden in the shadows of faith and fear.

The sun dipped behind the hills, casting a golden hue over the village. Asuran and Vettison sat in the opulent sitting room of the temporary bungalow Asuran had acquired for his stay in the village. The space, though ornate with expensive furnishings, seemed out of place amidst the rustic simplicity of the village. A knock on the door broke the silence.

"Come in," Asuran called, his voice sharp, expecting Taran.

Taran entered, his expression serious, carrying the weight of what he had discovered.

"Well, Taran," Asuran said, reclining on the plush sofa, "you've been sniffing around like a bloodhound. What have you found?"

Taran pulled a chair closer to the table where they sat. "The villagers don't know anything," he said bluntly.

Asuran raised an eyebrow. "What do you mean, *nothing*? Surely someone knows the truth about that land."

"They don't," Taran insisted. "I've spoken to several of them, including Kumarsen. Everyone has their own version of the curse. One says it's haunted by ancient warriors. Another claims sorcerers placed a hex on it. And then there's the theory about the gods marking it as sacred. None of it adds up."

Vettison leaned forward, his sharp eyes narrowing. "So they're just parroting old tales?"

"Exactly," Taran replied. "The only thing they agree on is their faith in Deva Neeladri. He's the one who warned them to stay away from the land. That's the only constant in all their stories."

Asuran frowned, tapping his fingers on the armrest. "Deva Neeladri," he repeated slowly, as though tasting the name. "The demigod."

Taran nodded. "Yes. If anyone knows the truth, it's him. But here's the problem—he's not exactly someone you can walk up to and question. He only communicates through Rayan, the village priest, during specific ceremonies. And even then, it's not like you can ask him anything you want."

Asuran smirked. "So you're saying the villagers are protecting a lie under the guise of faith?"

Taran shook his head. "No, they're not lying. They genuinely don't know. They've built their lives around Deva Neeladri's guidance. His word is law. They don't question it, they just obey."

"Convenient," Asuran muttered, exchanging a glance with Vettison.

"There's more," Taran continued. "Normally, Deva Neeladri speaks through Rayan during the annual festival. But if there's a serious issue—a life-threatening problem—villagers can perform a specific ritual to summon him.

Even then, it's not guaranteed he'll come. It's entirely up to him. Rayan has no control over it."

Vettison raised an eyebrow. "So Rayan himself doesn't know when or why Neeladri will take over his body?"

"Exactly," Taran confirmed. "Even Rayan is just a vessel. He's as much at the mercy of Neeladri's will as anyone else."

Asuran leaned back, folding his arms. His sharp features darkened with thought. "So, if we want answers, we have to get Neeladri to talk. But only the villagers can summon him. Is that what you're saying?"

"Yes," Taran replied. "If you want the truth about the land, Deva Neeladri is your only option. But convincing the villagers to summon him for your purposes? That's another matter entirely."

Asuran's eyes gleamed with a dangerous light. "We don't need to convince them. We just need to manipulate the circumstances. If this Neeladri only appears in times of dire need, then we create a 'dire need.'"

Taran stiffened. "What are you suggesting?"

"Think about it," Asuran said, his tone smooth and calculated. "We stage a situation that forces the villagers to call upon their god. Something that makes them believe their very survival depends on it. Once Neeladri is here, we find a way to steer the conversation toward the cursed land."

"That's risky," Taran said cautiously. "If they find out it's a setup—"

"They won't," Vettison interjected coldly. "Villagers are simple folk, Taran. They'll believe what we want them to believe."

Taran hesitated, glancing between the two men. "Even if you pull this off, how do you plan to get Neeladri to talk about the land? He doesn't owe you any answers."

Asuran's smile was thin and dangerous. "Oh, I think he'll answer. If he cares so much about this village, he'll do whatever it takes to protect it. And if that means revealing the truth about that land, then so be it."

"And if he doesn't?" Taran asked.

"Then we make him," Vettison said, his voice like ice.

Taran's stomach churned. He could see the ruthlessness in their eyes, the absolute determination to get what they wanted, no matter the cost. "You're playing with fire," he warned.

Asuran laughed, a low, mocking sound. "Fire? No, my friend. We're lighting a torch. And when this is all over, this village will finally step out of the dark ages and into prosperity. You'll see."

Taran said nothing, but unease settled over him like a heavy cloak. Asuran and Vettison were determined to uncover the truth about the cursed land, no matter the consequences. And as Taran left the bungalow that night, he couldn't shake the feeling that they were about to unleash something far more dangerous than they could imagine.

The tension in the air was palpable as Asuran Das and Vettison sat in their lavishly appointed office at the foothills of the mountains. They had decided to bring in reinforcements—experts who could unravel the so-called "mystery" of the cursed land. If they could disprove the myths and superstitions surrounding it, they could convince the villagers to move forward. The stakes were high. A 1,000-acre plot of flat land in the hills was too valuable to be left untouched, no matter how deep the villagers' faith ran.

Their chosen team consisted of three experts:

1. **Dr. Leela**, a renowned mythological researcher known for her critical analyses of ancient Indian folklore.

2. **Professor Sian**, an anthropologist with expertise in mountain cultures.

3. **Dr. Rohit Kumar**, a geologist with a deep understanding of Himalayan topography and the science behind barren lands.

The three experts were flown in and briefed in detail. Armed with books, research papers, and modern equipment, they began their investigation.

Dr. Leela immersed herself in the ancient lore of the village, pouring over faded texts and engaging with the elders who guarded the oral traditions. She pieced together fragmented stories of a curse that dated back centuries—tales of betrayal, sacred pacts, and divine wrath. Each account varied, but they shared a common theme: the villagers' deep reliance on their demigod, Neeladri, as a protector from calamities. Leela marveled at how these myths, though rich in cultural significance, were likely crafted to explain natural phenomena and instill communal discipline in an era devoid of scientific understanding. To her, the curse was a fabrication—a tool of control rather than a reality.

Professor Sian delved into the lives of the villagers, observing their rituals and understanding their history. He discovered that the reverence for Neeladri stemmed from centuries of survival against harsh conditions. The demigod wasn't just a figure of worship but a unifying force, a psychological anchor that gave the people hope amidst avalanches, bitter winters, and isolation. However, this unwavering faith had evolved into an unquestioning obedience, stifling any attempts to challenge traditional narratives. Bhattacharya noted how the villagers' dependence on Neeladri symbolized their struggle to reconcile their heritage with the demands of the modern world.

Dr. Rohit Kumar took a scientific approach, focusing on the land itself. Armed with advanced equipment, he analyzed soil samples and geological maps, revealing a barren patch that lacked essential nutrients and a shallow water table. While unusual in a region known for fertile valleys, this anomaly was purely natural. He found no evidence of a curse—just an inhospitable piece of earth shaped by millennia of geological processes. To Rohit, the myths surrounding the land were born out of ignorance and fear, perpetuated by a lack of understanding about the environment. The curse, he concluded, was nothing more than a compelling story masking a mundane reality.

Gathered in Asuran's office, the three experts delivered their consolidated analysis:

"Throughout history," Professor Bhattacharya began, "humans have created gods to cope with challenges. Mountains, in particular, were seen as the domain of divine beings because of their grandeur and unpredictability. These beliefs served a purpose—they united communities, provided hope during hardships, and explained phenomena that ancient people couldn't understand."

"But today," Dr. Leela continued, "we have the tools to understand our environment rationally. Myths and legends are valuable cultural artifacts, but they shouldn't hold people back. The villagers' attachment to Neeladri is understandable, but it's based on fear, not fact. They don't question because they're afraid of the consequences."

Dr. Rohit added, "And the so-called curse? It's just poor soil. This is a classic case of nature being misinterpreted as supernatural. There's no curse—just a lack of knowledge about the land's geological composition."

Professor Sian concluded, "We're not saying faith is unnecessary. We believe in God, too. Faith can coexist with progress. But a demigod speaking through a villager and dictating land use? That's a relic of a bygone era. The villagers must realize they have the power to decide their own destiny."

Asuran leaned forward, his eyes gleaming with satisfaction. "So what's the solution?"

Dr. Leela replied, "Educate the villagers. Show them that their fears are unfounded. Use science and logic to counter the myths. Convince them that developing the land is not an act of betrayal but a step toward a better future."

Professor Sian warned, "But tread carefully. If you're too aggressive, they'll cling to their faith even harder. Respect their beliefs, but guide them toward progress."

Dr. Rohit smiled. "And once they see the possibilities, they'll come around. That land isn't cursed—it's an opportunity waiting to be seized."

Asuran's grin widened. "Let's get to work, then."

And with that, the next phase of his plan began.

# The Bruise of Shadows

The winds howled like restless spirits, rattling the wooden shutters of Kumarsen's small hut. A cold draft seeped through the cracks, waking him from his sleep. His eyes fluttered open, and for a moment, he thought it was just another winter night. But something felt wrong. The air carried an unease that seeped into his bones.

He rose from his bed, drawn to the window by an inexplicable force. The moonless night outside was pitch black; the outlines of the pine trees barely visible against the swirling mist. Suddenly, a flicker of light caught his eye. Torches. A group of men was moving through the village, their shadows dancing ominously in the distance.

Kumarsen squinted, and his heart sank when he recognized two figures at the center of the group. Asuran and Vettison. What were they doing here at this hour? The villagers had gone to bed hours ago, yet this gathering felt deliberate, and secretive. Kumarsen tightened his shawl and slipped quietly out of his hut, following the faint murmur of voices.

He crept closer, his bare feet making no sound on the damp earth. From behind a wall, he listened intently, his heart pounding in his chest.

"Asuran," one villager's voice wavered, hesitant yet curious. "You're sure this will benefit all of us?"

"Of course," Asuran replied smoothly, his voice dripping with conviction. "This land has been idle for centuries, wasted on myths and fear. Imagine what we can achieve. Prosperity, growth, a future for your children. But we must act quickly. The longer we wait, the more we lose."

Vettison added, his tone persuasive, "We've already gained the support of Rayan and a few others. You'll see for yourself. This is the opportunity of a lifetime."

Kumarsen's blood ran cold. Rayan? The priest was practically the voice of the village's traditions. If they had swayed him, who else might have fallen under their spell? He dared a glance from behind the wall and saw the villagers nodding, their faces etched with uncertainty but also the glimmer of hope Asuran and Vettison were peddling.

The group began to move, heading toward the cursed land. Kumarsen trailed them, his steps careful and measured, his breath shallow. The further they walked, the more sinister the atmosphere became. The pine trees seemed to close in, their twisted branches clawing at the night sky. The animal cries in the distance grew louder, more frantic, as if warning him to turn back.

When they reached the outskirts of the cursed land, Kumarsen froze. A massive crane loomed in the darkness, its steel arm gleaming faintly under the torchlight. Other heavy machinery stood nearby, ominous and silent, waiting like predators ready to pounce.

The group advanced, the villagers now hesitant but still following Asuran and Vettison's lead. Kumarsen, staying hidden, edged closer. He watched in horror as the crane roared to life, its engine shattering the silence. Its claw dug into the earth with a deafening rumble, tearing into the sacred soil.

"No," Kumarsen whispered to himself, his fists clenching. "This cannot happen."

He stepped forward, his instincts urging him to intervene. Staying low, he moved closer to the workers. The flickering torchlight cast eerie shadows over the scene, making every step feel like a descent into darkness.

When he was just a few meters away, he saw **Rayan** standing near the edge of the excavation site, his face blank, almost trance-like. Kumarsen's heart broke. Was this truly Rayan?

A surge of courage overtook him. "Stop this madness!" he shouted, stepping into the light.

The workers turned, startled, but Asuran's commanding voice cut through the chaos. "Who dares interrupt?"

"It's Kumarsen!" one of the villagers exclaimed.

Kumarsen pushed through the group, his eyes blazing. "You cannot dig here! This land is sacred. You are inviting a wrath you cannot comprehend."

Asuran's smirk didn't falter. "Kumarsen, you've let old tales cloud your mind. Step aside. This is for the future of your village."

"I will not," Kumarsen growled. He lunged toward the machinery, desperate to shut it down. But before he could reach it, a burly worker stepped forward and struck him hard across the face. The force of the punch sent him sprawling to the ground, his vision blurring as pain exploded in his head.

Dazed, Kumarsen tried to rise, his legs trembling. He crawled toward the edge of the excavation pit, trying to catch his breath. Through his half-closed eyes, he saw Rayan standing eerily still, as if caught in some invisible grip. Behind him, in the distance, a figure appeared among the trees.

Kumarsen blinked, unsure if his mind was playing tricks on him. The figure was tall, shrouded in a faint blue glow, its piercing eyes watching the scene unfold. For a moment, Kumarsen felt a flicker of recognition.

"**Neeladri**," he whispered, his voice barely audible.

The figure seemed to tilt its head, observing. Kumarsen raised his hands in devotion, his heart both heavy and hopeful. But before he could utter another word, his body gave out, and he collapsed near the edge of the pit.

He woke with a start, drenched in sweat. The cold light of dawn seeped through the cracks in his hut. His hands trembled as he touched his face, half-expecting to find the bruise from the punch. But there was nothing.

"**A dream,**" he muttered, his voice shaky. "**Just a dream.**"

Yet the vividness of it lingered, the weight of it pressing on his chest. It didn't feel like a mere nightmare. It felt like a warning.

***

Kumarsen rubbed his eyes, the remnants of the haunting dream still clinging to his mind like a fog. The vividness of it all—the dark, moonless night, the crane tearing into the sacred land, and the punch that had sent him sprawling—refused to fade. Shaking his head, he dismissed it as an overactive imagination and got out of bed.

The chilly morning air bit at his skin as he shuffled to the washroom. Flicking on the light, he grabbed his toothbrush, applied a dollop of toothpaste, and began brushing motions. His mind drifted back to the dream, the vivid scenes replaying in his head.

When he glanced up into the mirror, his heart skipped a beat.

There, staring back at him, was not just his reflection but the unmistakable evidence of a bruise—a deep, purplish mark blooming on the left side of his face. His toothbrush froze mid-motion as his eyes widened in shock.

**"This can't be…"** he muttered, stepping closer to the mirror.

The bruise throbbed faintly, a painful reminder of something that shouldn't have been real. He touched it gently and winced.

**"How… how is this possible?"** Kumarsen whispered to himself. His hands gripped the edges of the sink as his mind raced.

It had only been a dream, hadn't it? He had never left his home, never confronted the group, and certainly never been punched. And yet, the evidence was right in front of him. His reflection mocked him with its reality.

The mirror seemed to magnify his confusion, the silence of the room pressing on him like a weight. He splashed water on his face, as though hoping to wash away the impossible. But the bruise remained.

Still dazed, Kumarsen decided to push the thoughts aside, convincing himself it was an odd coincidence or perhaps a fleeting memory of some forgotten incident. He needed milk and some air to clear his mind.

He grabbed his shawl and stepped out into the crisp morning. The village was beginning to stir, the faint sounds of birdsong mixing with the soft hum of activity. As he walked to the milk shop, he pulled the shawl closer around him, hoping to shield his face from prying eyes.

At the shop, a small crowd had gathered, exchanging pleasantries and chatting about the day ahead. The village locksmith, noticed Kumarsen as he approached.

"Kumarsen bhai!" He greeted warmly, his sharp eyes narrowing almost immediately as he caught sight of Kumarsen's face. "What happened to you? That bruise looks bad!"

Kumarsen hesitated, instinctively reaching up to touch his cheek. "Ah, it's nothing," he said, forcing a chuckle. "I slipped in my courtyard this morning. Fell right onto the edge of a pot."

The group of villagers, including the shopkeeper and a few others, leaned in closer, concern etched on their faces.

"You should be more careful," said an elderly woman who was known for her sharp tongue but warm heart. "At your age, a fall like that can be serious."

"I'm fine, really," Kumarsen assured them, waving his hand dismissively. "It looks worse than it is."

Blacksmith handed him a packet of milk but didn't seem convinced. "Well, if you say so," he said, though his tone was skeptical. "But you should put some turmeric on it. Bruises heal faster that way."

As the group began to disperse, the backsmith, Kaalan lingered, his voice dropping to a conspiratorial whisper. "Did you hear about the tourists asking questions about the cursed land?"

Kumarsen's heart skipped a beat, but he kept his expression neutral. "Tourists? What questions?"

Kaalan shrugged. "They've been poking around, asking about the stories and legends. Who knows what they're up to? Maybe they think they'll write a book or make a film. These outsiders, always curious about things they don't understand."

Elder Lady chimed in, her voice carrying an edge of disapproval. "Why do they care about our land? It's been this way for generations. Cursed or not, it's ours. They should leave it alone."

Another man,  added, "It's not just about curiosity. With all the young people leaving the hills for the cities, it's no surprise outsiders are starting to show interest. Did you see today's paper? Migration rates are at an all-time high. Half of our youth are gone, working in factories and offices down in the plains."

Meera shook her head sadly. "Can you blame them? There's nothing here for them. No jobs, no opportunities. And now these tourists come, asking about curses as if it's some story for their entertainment."

Kumarsen listened quietly, his mind racing. The conversation had taken an unexpected turn, but the mention of the cursed land felt like a thread pulling at the edges of his thoughts.

Prem continued, "It's true, though. Tourists are increasing every year. Some come for the mountains, some for the stories. They spend money, sure, but they also disrupt things. Now they're sniffing around the cursed land? That's bound to stir up trouble."

Lady sighed. "Let them dig if they want. It's their lives they're playing with, not ours."

Kumarsen's grip tightened on the milk packet as he listened. The villagers' words swirled around him, each one adding to the unease that had been growing since he'd woken up. The dream, the bruise, the tourists—it was all connected, but how?

"Maybe it's time we told them the truth," Blacksmith said suddenly, his voice low. "The real story of the curse."

Old lady snapped her head toward him, her eyes narrowing. "There is no 'real' story, Gokul. Just tales passed down to keep us safe. And they've done their job well enough, haven't they?"

The group fell silent, the weight of her words settling over them. Kumarsen took a deep breath and forced a smile.

"Well," he said, breaking the tension, "I should get back. Lots to do today."

As he walked away, the weight of their conversation hung heavy on his shoulders. The bruise on his face throbbed faintly, a physical reminder of the mysteries swirling around him. For the first time in years, Kumarsen felt like a stranger in his village. And the unease he carried was only growing.

In the evening, sunlight streamed weakly through the cracks in the wooden shutters of Kumarsen's home, casting long, diffused rays across the room. The faint aroma of incense lingered in the air, mingling with the earthy smell of the damp soil outside. Kumarsen sat cross-legged on the floor, sipping his tea thoughtfully. His mother, draped in a faded but clean shawl, stood by the stove, her sharp eyes studying him as she stirred the pot of lentils.

"You know," she began, her voice steady but edged with concern, "people in the village can't stop talking about the cursed land. Everywhere I go—at the well, at the temple, even the market—it's all they talk about." She paused, turning to face him. "And do you know what else they're saying? That it all started because of you."

Kumarsen looked up from his tea, startled.

"Because of me?" he asked, his brows furrowing.

"Yes," she replied firmly, crossing her arms over her chest. "Ever since you stood before Neeladri during the ceremony and asked about that cursed land, it's been on everyone's lips. You may not have meant to stir things up, but you did. And now this talk is spreading like wildfire."

Kumarsen placed his tea cup down carefully. His mother's words struck a chord. He thought back to that moment—standing before the demigod, the collective gaze of the villagers heavy upon him, and his bold question cutting through the sacred silence.

She continued, her tone softening slightly. "I even heard people say Asuran met with you soon after. What does he want? Why are people so restless about this cursed land now?"

Kumarsen sighed, leaning back against the wall. "I didn't mean for this to happen. I just thought... if I could understand why the land was cursed, maybe we could find some peace about it. Maybe even use it to help the village grow. But now…" He shook his head. "Now it feels like I've only made things worse."

His mother sat down beside him, her wrinkled hands resting on her lap. "Son, the land has always been a source of unease, but Neeladri's decree kept us safe. People trusted him, and they left it alone. Why did you need to ask? What did you plan to do with the answer, even if you got one?"

Kumarsen hesitated, running a hand through his hair. He hadn't thought this far. The question had come to him impulsively, a whisper of curiosity that he couldn't suppress.

"I thought maybe… just maybe, we were holding ourselves back because of old fears," he admitted quietly. "If the curse wasn't real, we could make use of that land. Do you know how much a thousand acres of flat, fertile land could mean to this village? Jobs, homes, food. Everything we struggle for could be solved."

His mother's eyes hardened. "And what if the curse *is* real? What if by asking, you've awakened something that should've been left alone?"

He didn't answer immediately. The weight of her words sank in, but so did a lingering doubt.

"And Asuran?" she pressed. "What does he want with you? He's not the kind of man to involve himself unless he sees something to gain. Did he push you to ask Neeladri about the land?"

"No," Kumarsen replied firmly. "He didn't. But... he came to me afterward. Tried to convince me that the land's curse is just a story, that we're wasting an opportunity."

His mother's lips tightened. "And what did you say?"

"I told him the land is sacred, and we can't go against Neeladri's word. But..." Kumarsen trailed off, guilt creeping into his voice. "It's true that since then, the village has been uneasy. People have started questioning things they wouldn't dare speak of before."

His mother shook her head slowly. "Curiosity is a dangerous thing, son. You've opened a door that might not be easy to close. The land has remained untouched for generations, and Neeladri has always protected us. If people lose their faith, what will happen to the village?"

Kumarsen looked away, his jaw tightening. "So, what do you want me to do? Pretend like I never asked. Ignore everything happening around us?"

His mother's voice softened. "No, I want you to think carefully about what you're doing. You've already shaken the balance. You need to figure out if you're prepared to face whatever comes next. But one thing is certain—if you challenge Neeladri, you won't just be questioning a curse. You'll be questioning the very foundation of this village."

The room fell silent except for the faint bubbling of the pot on the stove. Outside, the chirping of birds signalled the dusk of the day.

"I didn't mean for this to happen," he said again, almost to himself. "I just wanted to help."

His mother reached out, placing a comforting hand on his arm. "Sometimes, the path to helping others is knowing when to let things be. But if you truly feel there's more to this, then you must tread carefully, Kumarsen. The land may be cursed, or it may not be. But you're walking into a storm, and storms don't care about intentions."

Kumarsen nodded, though his heart was heavy. The words of Neeladri echoed in his mind, but so did the questions Asuran had planted. The truth awaited somewhere in the tangled web of fear, tradition, and ambition. And Kumarsen wasn't sure if he was ready to face it.

***

The wooden beams of Kumarsen's modest home creaked as a gust of wind pushed against the walls. Kumarsen sat at the edge of his bed, head buried in his hands, his breathing uneven. The bruises on his cheek throbbed faintly—a reminder of his dream that refused to fade. Was it even a dream?

The events of the past days played over in his mind like an unsettling song he couldn't escape. He had asked about the cursed land during the ceremony. Asuran had come to him soon after, subtly probing his thoughts. And now, the villagers were whispering, questioning things they had never dared before.

And that dream…

Kumarsen shivered, even though the room was warm. The sight of the crane digging into the land, the confrontation with Asuran and Rayan, and the glimpse of that figure—was it really Neeladri, watching from the shadows? And the bruise—how could something from a dream leave a mark on his face?

"This doesn't make sense," he muttered aloud.

He got up and paced the small room, his bare feet thudding softly against the wooden floor. His mother's earlier words echoed in his head: ***You've opened a door that might not be easy to close.***

Had he? Was he responsible for all of this?

His thoughts spiraled further. Asuran's visit had been too convenient, too timed. He had acted supportive, but his words had planted doubts in Kumarsen's mind. Was he manipulating him? Using him as a pawn?

"I need answers," Kumarsen said, his voice firmer now.

But where would he start? The cursed land was forbidden. The villagers wouldn't talk. And Neeladri…

He shook his head. The idea of confronting the demigod seemed impossible.

His eyes fell on the faint reflection of himself in the small mirror above his dresser. He stepped closer, staring at the bruise on his face. His fingers lightly traced it, and he winced at the tenderness.

"This isn't just a dream," he whispered.

A chill ran down his spine as another thought crept in: *What if Neeladri wanted me to see this?*

The idea both terrified and intrigued him. If the demigod was truly watching, then perhaps he was also waiting for Kumarsen to act.

"Enough," he said, slamming his hand against the dresser. The sound reverberated in the small room, jolting him back to focus.

He needed to stop overthinking and start searching for the truth.

The night was deep and silent when Kumarsen finally left his home. The village was still, save for the faint chirping of crickets. A sliver of moonlight illuminated the cobbled paths, casting eerie shadows that stretched and shifted with each step.

He made his way to the outskirts of the village, where the cursed land lay beyond the line of towering pine trees. The air grew colder as he approached, the scent of damp earth and pine needles sharp in his nostrils.

He paused at the edge of the treeline, hesitating. The dark expanse of the forbidden land loomed before him, and for a moment, fear gripped his chest. But the bruises on his face reminded him of the unanswered questions gnawing at his mind.

With a deep breath, he stepped forward, his feet crunching on the dry leaves.

The next day, Kumarsen sat in the small tea shop at the heart of the village, his hands wrapped around a steaming cup of tea. His night had been fruitless—no signs of the crane, no disturbances. Just the oppressive silence of the cursed land.

As he stared blankly into his cup, a familiar voice interrupted his thoughts.

"Kumarsen," said a man, pulling up a stool across from him. It was Kaalan, the village Blacksmith. "You look like you haven't slept."

Kumarsen forced a smile. "Just tired, that's all."

Kaalan chuckled. "Well, you're not alone. Half the village seems restless these days." He leaned in slightly, lowering his voice. "You know, people are talking about the cursed land again. First time in decades."

Kumarsen's grip on his cup tightened. "Really? What are they saying?"

"Oh, all sorts of things," Kaalan said, waving his hand. "Some say the land's waking up because the villagers have angered Neeladri. Others think it's a sign that we need to use it before it's too late."

Kumarsen frowned. "And you? What do you think?"

Kaalan shrugged. "I think we're just scared of change. That land's been untouched for so long it's become more of a story than a reality. But who knows? Maybe the stories are true."

The conversation was interrupted by the arrival of an elderly woman selling vegetables. She joined their table, her weathered face serious.

"Kumarsen," she said, her voice low, "you've stirred something by asking Neeladri about the land."

He stiffened. "I didn't mean to cause trouble."

"It's not about trouble," she replied. "It's about the balance. The land has its place in our village's history. If you disturb it…" She trailed off, her eyes darkening.

Kumarsen felt the weight of her words but also the rising determination within him. Whatever the truth, he needed to find it—if only to bring peace to himself and the village.

By evening, Kumarsen sat alone near the edge of the cursed land, staring out at the dark expanse. His thoughts were a storm, but one thing was clear: he couldn't let fear or guilt hold him back.

He didn't know what awaited him, but he knew one thing: he would uncover the secrets of the cursed land, no matter the cost.

***

The morning sun bathed the village in a gentle golden light, casting long shadows over the cobblestone paths. Kumarsen sat on the stone bench near the well, the cool breeze carrying the faint scent of dew-soaked earth. Yet, his mind remained a storm of confusion and unanswered questions. The events of the past days weighed heavily on him—his dream, the bruise, the whispers of the villagers, and the strange unease that seemed to linger in the air like an unwelcome guest.

As he absently traced the edge of his wooden staff, the sound of approaching footsteps broke his reverie. Kumarsen looked up, squinting against the sunlight, to see Taran, the tourist-turned-researcher, striding toward him with an urgency that couldn't be ignored.

"Kumarsen," Taran called, his voice steady but carrying a note of hesitation.

"What is it now, Taran?" Kumarsen asked, his eyes narrowing.

Taran hesitated, then sat beside him. He glanced around as if ensuring no one was eavesdropping.

"I need to tell you the truth," he said, lowering his voice.

"The truth about what?" Kumarsen asked, his tone guarded.

"About why I came to this village." Taran's expression was serious, almost pleading. "It wasn't just curiosity about the cursed land."

Kumarsen's grip on his staff tightened. "Go on."

Taran exhaled heavily. "Asuran and Vettison sent me here."

Kumarsen's eyes darkened, and his posture stiffened. "What are you saying?"

"They hired me to gather information about the cursed land," Taran confessed. "They knew the villagers wouldn't talk to outsiders like them, but they thought you might open up to someone like me. My job was to figure out what's true, what's just a story, and whether there's anything that could stop them from getting what they want."

Kumarsen stood abruptly, his jaw clenched. "So, you're just another one of their pawns?"

"No," Taran said quickly, standing as well. "That's not what I want. I swear to you, Kumarsen, I had no idea how deep this went until I came here. And now that I've seen the village, spoken to the people, I can't do what they want."

Kumarsen's glare softened slightly, but suspicion lingered in his voice. "Why are you telling me this now?"

"Because I respect these mountains," Taran said firmly. "And the people who live here. I may have come here under false pretenses, but I've come to believe there's something worth protecting. Something real."

Kumarsen studied him for a long moment, his eyes searching for any sign of deception. Finally, he sat back down, motioning for Taran to do the same.

"Tell me everything," Kumarsen said.

Taran spoke at length, detailing Asuran and Vettison's grand plans for the cursed land—a sprawling housing society, complete with modern amenities. He explained how they believed the stories of the curse were mere superstition, an obstacle to be overcome with logic and research.

"They've already hired experts," Taran said. "A mythological researcher, an anthropologist, and a geologist. They're working on reports to disprove the curse, to make the land seem like just another plot of earth."

Kumarsen frowned. "And what do these experts think?"

Taran shrugged. "The geologist says the land is barren but stable. The anthropologist claims the stories are just cultural relics, passed down to maintain order. And the mythological researcher—well, he thinks it's all symbolic. A way for the villagers to cope with fear."

"And what do you think?" Kumarsen asked, his gaze piercing.

Taran hesitated, then said, "I think there's more to this than anyone realizes. Whether the curse is real or not, it's clear that this land means something to the people here. It's not just a piece of dirt—it's a part of their lives, their identity."

Kumarsen leaned back, his expression unreadable. "And what do you want from me?"

"I want to help you," Taran said simply. "To find the truth—not just about the curse, but about what this land really holds. I don't trust Asuran and Vettison, and I don't think they'll stop until they get what they want. But if we work together, we might be able to stay ahead of them."

Kumarsen looked away, his eyes scanning the distant hills. The weight of responsibility pressed heavily on his shoulders. He didn't know whether to trust Taran, but he couldn't deny that the young man seemed genuine. And Kumarsen couldn't do this alone.

"Fine," Kumarsen said finally. "But if you're lying to me, Taran, I'll make sure the entire village knows who you're working for."

"I'm not lying," Taran said earnestly.

"Then let's get started," Kumarsen said, his voice firm. "But we do this my way."

***

The evening air was thick with the mingling scents of incense and freshly lit oil lamps. The temple courtyard glowed softly under the faint light of lanterns strung around its perimeter. The echo of the evening pooja's chants still lingered, a hum of devotion stretching beyond the sacred space. Kumarsen, with Taran by his side, approached Rayan, who was closing the temple gates for the night.

Rayan, a tall, wiry man with a face weathered by years of worship and the weight of being the vessel of Deva Neeladri, turned to greet them. His gaze was warm yet firm, reflecting his dual roles as spiritual guide and the custodian of the villagers' faith.

"Rayan," Kumarsen began cautiously, his voice steady but laden with urgency, "we need to talk."

Rayan raised an eyebrow, sensing the gravity in Kumarsen's tone. "What troubles you, Kumarsen? The pooja has brought peace to the temple tonight. Shouldn't it have done the same for your soul?"

Kumarsen exchanged a glance with Taran before stepping closer. "It's about the land," he said, lowering his voice to avoid attracting attention from the few remaining worshippers. "The cursed land."

Rayan's expression darkened instantly, his calm demeanor giving way to visible disapproval. "That land again?" His voice rose sharply, enough to make Kumarsen flinch. "Did you not hear Deva Neeladri's warning during the ceremony? He spoke clearly—no one is to discuss or meddle with that land!"

"I heard him," Kumarsen replied, his tone respectful but firm. "But the village is restless, Rayan. People are talking. And now, with these strangers in the village…" He gestured toward Taran. "I need to understand what we're dealing with—for the safety of everyone."

Rayan turned his stern gaze to Taran, eyes narrowing. "And who is this outsider you've brought into our affairs?"

Taran stepped forward, bowing slightly. "My name is Taran," he said, his tone calm but earnest. "I came here to learn about the village and its history. I didn't intend to get involved in anything beyond that, but I've seen how much this land means to everyone here. I want to help Kumarsen find the truth—not to disrupt your faith, but to protect it."

Rayan crossed his arms, his skepticism evident. "Protect it? Outsiders like you don't understand what you're meddling with. This village has lived in harmony because we've obeyed Neeladri's commands. You think you can unravel centuries of faith with your curiosity?"

Kumarsen stepped in before the tension escalated further. "Rayan, please. This isn't about questioning Neeladri's power. But the village is changing. Outsiders are asking questions, people are starting to doubt, and fear is spreading. If we don't find the truth—whatever it may be—we risk losing not just the land, but the unity of our people."

Rayan's features softened slightly, though his distrust remained. He sighed deeply. "The land's curse is not a story to uncover; it's a warning to heed. What Neeladri has forbidden, no man should challenge. You're treading dangerous ground, Kumarsen."

"I know the risks," Kumarsen replied. "But if there's even a chance that we can protect the village better by understanding the curse, isn't it worth trying? We owe it to the people to ensure their safety in every way."

Rayan looked between Kumarsen and Taran, his expression a mixture of frustration and concern. Finally, he spoke, his voice low and measured. "I cannot go against Neeladri's command. But if you insist on this path, proceed with respect and caution. The land is not just cursed—it's sacred in ways we may never fully understand."

Taran nodded, a glimmer of determination in his eyes. "Thank you, Rayan. We'll be careful. Our goal is to protect, not to harm."

Rayan shook his head, worry etched into his features. "Be careful that your curiosity doesn't awaken forces you cannot control," he warned. "And Kumarsen… remember where your loyalties lie."

Kumarsen nodded, the weight of Rayan's words pressing heavily on his shoulders. As they turned to leave, Rayan called out, his voice softer now but still tinged with urgency.

"There's one more thing," Rayan said, stepping closer. "If you truly seek answers, there is someone who might help you. An old priest, now living as a yogi in the Nandan mountains. He was one of the three main priests of this temple twenty-five years ago. He left the village after… certain events. If anyone holds secrets about the land and its curse, it's him."

Kumarsen's eyes widened. "Why haven't you mentioned this before?"

"Because some secrets are better left buried," Rayan said solemnly. "But if you are determined to dig, you must be prepared for what you might find. Seek him, but know this—what he reveals could change everything you think you know about this village, its god, and that land."

Kumarsen and Taran exchanged a glance, the weight of their task growing heavier. The evening air seemed colder now, the shadows of the temple stretching long and dark as they left, carrying Rayan's words with them like a burden—and a challenge.

The crisp mountain air carried a chill as Kumarsen and Taran began their journey toward the Nandan mountains. The narrow trail snaked upward, flanked by towering pines on one side and sheer cliffs on the other. Their footsteps crunched against the gravel, a rhythmic echo in the quiet expanse of wilderness. The early morning sun painted the peaks in hues of gold, casting long shadows in the valley below.

"This feels surreal," Taran remarked, adjusting his backpack. "It's hard to imagine people have lived in these mountains for centuries. The sheer isolation, the quiet… it's overwhelming."

Kumarsen glanced at him. "It's not just isolation. For us, the mountains are sacred. Every tree, every stream, every rock—there's a story woven into them. It's why Neeladri means so much to us."

"And now we're walking into another story," Taran said with a faint smile, though his tone carried an undercurrent of seriousness.

The trail grew steeper as they ascended, the path narrowing to a precarious edge. Below them, a roaring stream cut through the valley like a silver thread. They stopped to catch their breath near a small shrine nestled in the crook of a cliffside.

The shrine was modest—a stone structure adorned with faded red cloth and marigold garlands. A brass bell hung from the roof, swaying gently in the breeze. Taran knelt to inspect it, his fingers brushing against the carvings etched into the stone.

"This must be centuries old," he murmured.

Kumarsen rang the bell softly, the sound resonating across the mountains. "It's said that travelers leave their prayers here for safe passage."

They resumed their trek, the terrain becoming more challenging with each step. Thick patches of forest enveloped them, the sunlight filtering through the dense canopy in dappled patterns. The air was filled with the earthy scent of moss and pine, interspersed with the distant sound of waterfalls.

Night fell quickly in the mountains, bringing with it a biting cold. They set up camp near a small clearing, lighting a fire to ward off the chill. Over a simple meal of flatbread and dried fruits, the two shared their thoughts.

"Do you think this yogi will even talk to us?" Taran asked, watching the flames dance.

"If he's truly the priest Rayan mentioned, he'll listen," Kumarsen replied, his voice firm. "The question is whether he'll tell us what we need to know."

The fire crackled, its embers glowing like stars against the dark. The silence of the mountains was profound, broken only by the occasional rustle of leaves or the call of an owl.

### The Second Day

By dawn, they were back on the trail, their breaths visible in the frosty air. The path now wound through a series of ridges, each offering breathtaking views of snow-capped peaks in the distance. The sun cast long shadows over the rugged landscape, its warmth a welcome contrast to the biting cold.

They passed through meadows dotted with wildflowers, their vibrant colors a striking contrast against the muted greens and browns of the mountains. At one point, they encountered a herd of goats shepherded by an old man who greeted them with a toothless smile.

"Where are you headed?" the shepherd asked, leaning on his staff.

"To the Nandan peak," Kumarsen replied. "We're looking for a yogi who lives there."

The shepherd's expression grew somber. "The yogi… he's a recluse. Rarely seen. Lives beyond where most dare to go."

Kumarsen nodded. "We have to find him. It's important."

The shepherd offered a shrug and pointed toward the farthest ridge. "If you're determined, follow the trail past the pine grove. But be warned—it's a lonely path."

By midday, the weather began to shift. Clouds rolled in, casting a gray pall over the mountains. The wind picked up, carrying with it the faint promise of snow. The trail became more treacherous, forcing them to tread carefully.

At last, they reached a plateau that overlooked a deep valley. The view was breathtaking—a cascade of waterfalls tumbled down the cliffs, feeding into a crystalline lake below. Above it all, the jagged peaks of the Nandan range loomed, their snow-covered crests glistening like shards of glass.

"This is it," Kumarsen said, his voice tinged with awe. "Rayan said the yogi lives somewhere near the edge."

They searched tirelessly, their boots crunching through the thin layer of frost that covered the ground. The air was thin, each breath a labor. They found signs of habitation—a circle of stones that might have once held a fire, a makeshift shelter carved into the rock—but no sign of the yogi himself.

As the day waned, the first flakes of snow began to fall, dusting the landscape in white. Taran pulled his scarf tighter around his face. "We can't stay here much longer. It's going to snow heavily soon."

Kumarsen's gaze swept the horizon, his frustration mounting. "He has to be here. Rayan wouldn't have sent us if he wasn't."

"But what if he's moved on? Or…" Taran hesitated, not wanting to voice his darker thoughts.

The wind howled around them, and the snow intensified. Reluctantly, they retreated to a sheltered outcrop, setting up their camp for the night.

As the snow fell silently around them, Kumarsen stared out into the white expanse, his mind racing. "Why would Rayan send us here if the yogi couldn't help us?"

Taran shrugged, his hands extended toward the small fire they'd managed to light. "Maybe the yogi is a myth, like the stories about the land. Or maybe he's testing us, making sure we're truly determined."

Kumarsen's eyes narrowed, determination hardening his features. "We'll find him," he said, more to himself than to Taran. "We have to."

The mountains seemed to watch them in silence, their secrets buried deep beneath layers of snow and stone.

Kumarsen and Taran trudged through the fresh blanket of snow, the biting wind cutting through their layers of clothing. Each step felt heavier than the last, their boots sinking into the icy terrain. The silence of the mountains was only broken by the occasional creak of bending trees or the distant howl of the wind.

Exhaustion painted their faces as the relentless journey took its toll. The breathtaking beauty of the peaks, cloaked in glistening white, had lost its charm to their weary eyes. They reached a clearing where a massive pine tree stood tall, its branches heavy with snow. Beside it, a large stone offered a semblance of shelter.

"This is hopeless," Taran muttered, dropping his pack onto the ground. "We've searched every corner. The yogi either doesn't exist or doesn't want to be found."

Kumarsen, equally drained, sank onto the cold stone. His breath came out in visible puffs as he looked up at the darkening sky. "We can't give up. Not now. Not after coming so far."

"Let's rest," Taran suggested, leaning back against the tree. "The snow's not letting up, and we won't get far in this light."

Reluctantly, Kumarsen nodded. They huddled close to conserve warmth, the thick trunk of the pine shielding them from the worst of the wind. Sleep came gradually, their exhaustion overriding the discomfort of the cold.

A gentle but firm touch on Kumarsen's shoulder jolted him awake. His eyes fluttered open, and for a moment, he couldn't tell if he was still dreaming. Before him stood an old man, his face nearly obscured by a wild tangle of hair, mustache, and beard. His eyes, sharp and piercing, glinted like embers in the dim light of the snowy evening.

"What are you doing here?" the man asked, his voice deep and resonant. "The weather here is merciless. This is no place for tourists."

Taran stirred awake, his eyes widening at the sight of the figure before them. "Who are you?" he asked, his voice laced with awe and caution.

The old man gave a small, enigmatic smile. "I could ask you the same. Few venture into these mountains, especially in weather like this."

Kumarsen rose slowly, his body aching from the cold. "We came here looking for someone—a priest who once served in the temple near my village. They said he became a yogi and now lives in these mountains."

The old man's expression remained unreadable, but his gaze softened. "And why would you seek such a man? What questions haunt you so deeply that you would risk your lives to find him?"

Kumarsen hesitated. The weight of his quest—the dreams, the whispers, the bruises, the unease in the village—all surged through his mind. "I need answers," he said finally, his voice steady. "About the cursed land in my village. About Neeladri. About why the past seems to follow us no matter how far we try to move forward."

The old man looked at him for a long moment before stepping closer. "You've come far, and you've endured much. That shows strength… and perhaps a touch of foolishness."

Taran interjected, his curiosity bubbling over. "Do you know the priest we're looking for? Can you help us?"

The old man's gaze shifted to Taran, and for the first time, his lips curled into a faint smile. "You've already found him."

Both Kumarsen and Taran froze, disbelief etched on their faces.

"You?" Kumarsen asked, his voice barely above a whisper. "You're the priest? The one Rayan spoke of?"

The man nodded, the movement slow and deliberate. "I was a priest once, yes. But that life ended long ago. Now, I live here, among the mountains and their silence."

"Why did you leave?" Taran asked, unable to contain his curiosity.

The old man turned his gaze to the horizon, where the last light of the day cast a faint glow over the peaks. "That is a story for another time. For now, tell me what you seek, and I will decide if your questions deserve answers."

Kumarsen stepped forward, his eyes locking with the yogi's. "We need to know the truth about the land. The curse, the stories, the fears—they've held my village in their grip for generations. I need to understand what's real and what's not."

The yogi studied him intently, his piercing eyes seeming to delve into Kumarsen's very soul. Finally, he nodded. "Very well. But know this—seeking the truth comes at a cost. You may not like what you find."

Kumarsen's jaw tightened. "I'm ready to face it."

The yogi gestured for them to follow. "Come. There is a place where we can speak, away from the cold."

As they walked, the wind seemed to calm, and the snowfall lightened. The yogi led them to a small cave carved into the mountainside, its entrance sheltered by overhanging rock. Inside, a modest fire burned, its warmth a welcome reprieve from the icy outdoors.

They settled around the fire, the flickering flames casting dancing shadows on the cave walls. The yogi looked at them both, his expression grave. "You seek answers. But are you prepared for the burden of knowing?"

Kumarsen nodded, his resolve unwavering. "I have to be."

"Then listen carefully," the yogi said, his voice low and steady. "The land you speak of holds many secrets. Some are rooted in truth, others in fear. To understand it, you must be willing to confront both."

As the fire crackled softly, the three men sat in the heart of the mountains, the weight of their quest pressing heavily upon them.

***

The yogi leaned forward, his face shadowed by his thick beard as the dying embers of the fire flickered. The scent of burning pine needles filled the cold mountain air. Kumarsen and Taran sat in rapt silence, waiting for him to begin. When he spoke, his voice was low, each word weighted with the gravity of untold years.

“What I am about to tell you, is not something I saw with my own eyes, nor something anyone alive has witnessed. It is a story passed down, from my grandfather, and perhaps his grandfather before him. But stories are the soul of these mountains. They hold truths in their own way.”

He paused, gazing beyond them into the dark expanse of the Nandan mountains. Then, he continued.

“More than three hundred years ago, a man came to these mountains. He was not from here—he was from the plains, where life is flat, fertile, and warm. He brought with him his wife and two young children, a boy and a girl. They were poor, driven from their home by hunger and misfortune. When he reached this land, the endless stretch of untouched plains between the mountains must have seemed like a promise, a sanctuary. He decided to stay.

"The man worked tirelessly. He built a small hut for his family, using stone for the terrace and wooden planks for the walls. It wasn’t much, but it was shelter. He tilled the land, digging out the rocks with his bare hands, and planted seeds. His wife and children helped as much as they could, their hands as calloused and worn as his. They carved out a life, slowly but surely.

"For a while, it seemed they might find peace. The land rewarded their efforts. Crops sprouted, and they harvested just enough to survive. The children laughed again, running barefoot through the fields. For the first time in years, they felt like they had a place of their own."

The yogi's voice darkened. "But the mountains are not kind to the unwary. Life here is a balance, one that even the strongest struggle to maintain. The seasons shifted, and the rains turned relentless. The river swelled, and the winds screamed through the valley like wild beasts. The family's little hut creaked and shuddered against the storm, but it held—for now.

"The man and his family faced challenges beyond the weather. Wild animals circled their home at night, their glowing eyes visible in the darkness. The forests were dense and unfamiliar, their paths treacherous. And the land, though vast, was cruel. Soil that seemed fertile one season became barren the next. Crops failed. Hunger returned, gnawing at their resolve."

The yogi's eyes gleamed as he continued. "His children began to weaken. First, the little boy grew pale, coughing endlessly as the cold seeped into his bones. Then the girl fell ill, too. She would shiver even when wrapped in blankets. His wife was no better, always fevered, unable to gather strength. The man tried to care for them, but he himself grew thin, his hands trembling from exhaustion.

"Without food, their bodies could not heal. They were trapped in a cruel cycle: sickness bred weakness, and weakness prevented them from escaping their plight."

Kumarsen shifted uncomfortably, the yogi's words striking a chord deep within him. "So what did the man do?" he asked, his voice almost a whisper.

The yogi looked at him sharply, his expression unreadable. "What any desperate father would do. He sought help. But remember, the mountains were not like they are now. There were no roads, no hospitals, no markets. The nearest village was miles away, separated by treacherous terrain. Still, he left his family behind and journeyed to the village.

"The people there were kind in their way, but they had their own struggles. They offere d him food and advice but little else. One elder, however, told him to visit the temple and speak with the priest. 'The gods of these mountains are powerful,' the elder said. 'If you cannot fight the elements, then you must make peace with them."

The yogi leaned closer to the fire, his face glowing orange in its light. "The man went to the temple, a place older than any of the villages. He found the priest, an old man with a voice as deep as the mountains themselves. The priest listened to his story in silence. When the man finished, the priest spoke.

"'What you seek is balance,' the priest said. 'Balance with the mountains, balance with the land. These mountains are alive, and they watch those who dwell here. A Havan—a sacred fire ritual—might restore harmony. But you must understand, this is no guarantee. The mountains cannot be tamed, only respected.'"

Kumarsen frowned, his mind racing. "Did he, do it? The Havan?"

The yogi nodded. "He did. He returned to the village and gathered what little he could: firewood, herbs, grains, and milk. The villagers gave what they could spare. Then, he returned to his land, to his family, and prepared for the ritual.

The yogi's voice grew quieter, deeper, as if the very act of retelling the story demanded respect. Kumarsen and Taran leaned in, their breath visible in the cold air. The fire crackled softly between them, the night pressing close around the small circle of light.

"The man," the yogi continued, "was desperate, his hope flickering like a candle in the wind. With his wife and children too weak to move, he built the sacred altar himself, stone by stone. He gathered what the priest had instructed: ghee for the fire, water from the stream, handfuls of earth from the land, and fresh leaves to purify the space. For two days and nights, he worshipped without rest. He prayed not to one god, but to all five elements—the forces that bind our world together. Agni, the fire, to burn away their suffering. Jal, the water, to heal and sustain. Vayu, the air, to bring them life. Prithvi, the earth, to provide for them. And Akasha, the vast sky, to guide their spirits."

"In the cold embrace of the mountains, the ritual began," he continued. "On the first night, he lit the sacred fire, its light cutting through the oppressive darkness. 'Agni!' he cried, his voice hoarse but resolute. 'Consume our despair. Protect my family from harm.' The fire roared to life as if answering him, its flames stretching unnaturally high into the sky.

"As dawn approached, he turned to Jal, offering water from the river in a copper vessel. He poured it carefully around the altar, pleading, 'Cleanse us, O Jal. Heal the sickness that grips my children. Let your flow bring us new life.' The water seeped into the soil, vanishing as if the earth itself drank it greedily."

Kumarsen's chest tightened as the yogi spoke, his words heavy with an almost tangible power. Taran whispered, "It's as if the elements were listening."

The yogi glanced at him, his expression unreadable. "Perhaps they were," he said simply before continuing.

"By the second night, the man was exhausted. His hands trembled, his knees buckled, but he refused to stop. He turned to Vayu, the air that filled their lungs and whipped through the valley. Raising his arms, he called, 'Vayu! Carry away our pain. Fill this land with life and breath once more.' The winds howled in response, fierce and unyielding. It was as if the mountains themselves were testing his resolve."

The yogi's voice grew softer, drawing the listeners in closer. "Next, he knelt upon the earth, his fingers clawing into the soil. 'Prithvi,' he begged, 'you have cradled us, sheltered us. Let us give back to you. Teach me how to live in harmony with you.' He pressed his forehead to the ground, his tears soaking into the dirt.

"Finally, as the second dawn broke, he raised his eyes to the vast sky above. The stars faded into the light of morning, but he kept his gaze steady. 'Akasha,' he whispered, his voice barely audible, 'I seek your guidance. Help me see beyond the struggle. Show me a path to save my family.'"

Kumarsen shivered, not from the cold but from the weight of the story. "And then?" he asked.

The yogi's face darkened, shadows dancing across his features. "Then, the mountain spoke back."

Taran blinked, his brow furrowed in confusion. "What do you mean, the mountain spoke back?"

The yogi tilted his head, his gaze sharp. "What I mean is that the land is alive in ways we cannot understand. It watches, it listens, and sometimes—only sometimes—it answers. As the man completed his final prayer, the air grew unnaturally still. The fire did not die but froze, its flames rigid like molten glass. The ground beneath him trembled, not violently, but just enough to make him aware.

"Then came the voice—a low, guttural hum that seemed to rise from the depths of the earth itself. It was not a language he understood, yet he felt its meaning. A warning, perhaps. Or a promise. No one knows for sure."

Kumarsen leaned forward, his heart pounding. "What did the man do? Did he survive?"

The yogi sighed deeply, the sound heavy with unspoken sorrow. "He returned to his family. For a time, their health improved. The land seemed to provide once more. But **the man never spoke of what he experienced during those two days of worship**. He avoided the altar he had built, never lighting the fire again. The villagers who had helped him began to notice changes in the valley. The air seemed heavier, the animals more restless. The land had accepted his plea—**but at what cost?"**

The yogi's voice softened, taking on a tone of bittersweet nostalgia. Kumarsen and Taran sat frozen, the flickering flames casting long shadows across their faces.

"After that man's prayers, life began to change," the yogi began again, his eyes gazing into the fire as if it held the memories of centuries. "The harsh winters that once claimed lives grew more forgiving. The soil became richer and more fertile. Crops thrived—barley, maize, millet—each harvests more bountiful than the last. River flowed stronger and purer, their water shimmering as though blessed by some unseen force. It was as if the land had awakened, giving back what it had long withheld."

"And the man's family?" Taran asked.

"They grew strong," the yogi replied. "The children, once frail and sickly, ran through the fields with laughter that echoed through the valley. The wife's health returned, her face no longer pale but glowing with life. The man himself became a symbol of resilience, his struggles forgotten in the face of newfound prosperity. Other families, hearing of the transformation, began to arrive. They built homes, cleared fields, and planted their roots in this miraculous land."

The yogi paused, his expression hard to read. "Soon, it was no longer a solitary family, but a village. Small at first, with only a handful of huts dotting the hillside, but it grew. People came from far and wide, drawn by stories of abundance. The land seemed to welcome them, its bounty endless. Seasons flowed smoothly—warm summers, gentle monsoons, and winters that no longer threatened but nurtured. Peace reigned."

Kumarsen tilted his head, confused. "But if everything became so perfect, where does the curse fit into all this?"

The yogi held up a hand, silencing him. "Patience, Kumarsen. **Even in paradise, shadows lurk where light is brightest.**"

He continued, "With prosperity came tradition. The people, grateful for the blessings they believed had been bestowed upon them, began an annual ceremony. They gathered in the heart of the village, at the altar the man had once built. A grand pooja to honor the elements—the fire, the water, the earth, the air, and the sky. Offerings were made with reverence, their gratitude filling the valley like a hymn. For decades, this ceremony became the heartbeat of the village. It unified them, reminding all who lived there of the delicate balance that governed their lives."

The flames crackled loudly, startling Kumarsen. "It sounds... perfect," he murmured, though a sense of unease began to creep into his mind.

"It was," the yogi admitted. "For a time. The children grew into strong adults, and their children after them. The land thrived. The people thrived. But perfection has its price."

"What price?" Taran pressed, his voice barely a whisper.

The yogi's face darkened. "Prosperity breeds complacency. And in their comfort, the villagers forgot the most important lesson the man had learned—the land does not give without taking something in return."

He stopped speaking, letting his words hang ominously in the air. Kumarsen and Taran exchanged anxious glances, the flickering firelight unable to chase away the chill that had settled in their bones.

The yogi's voice lowered as if he were afraid the mountains themselves might overhear him. Kumarsen and Taran leaned in, their breaths visible in the cold night air. The fire sputtered, its light throwing long, flickering shadows over the three men.

"Years passed," the yogi began, "and the village flourished. But as with all things in life, the wheel turned. The bounty began to dwindle. Slowly at first—a smaller harvest here, an unusually harsh winter there. But soon, the change became undeniable. The winters grew brutal, unforgiving. Crops withered before they could fully grow, and streams that once ran strong began to dry. Livestock fell ill, and sickness spread among the villagers."

He paused, the crackle of the fire filling the silence. "The people turned to the annual pooja for salvation. They prayed harder, offered more, and pleaded for the elements' mercy. But it was as if their prayers fell on deaf ears. No matter how grand the ceremony, their situation grew worse."

Taran frowned. "Didn't they question why the pooja stopped working?"

The yogi nodded. "Oh, they questioned. And their questions soon turned to fear. Fear became desperation, and desperation sought a scapegoat. They turned to the First man who had led them into this life—the first settler, the one who had once been their symbol of hope and resilience."

Kumarsen felt a shiver crawl down his spine. "What did they do?"

"They gathered," the yogi said. "On the coldest night of the harshest winter, they gathered outside his home."

The scene shifted in Kumarsen's mind as the yogi described it.

The wind howled through the village, carrying with it the bitter chill of a night colder than any they had known.

Snow fell heavily, blanketing the huts and muffling the anguished cries of children within. The villagers, wrapped in layers of tattered wool, trudged through the knee-deep snow toward the man's house.

His home, once a symbol of triumph over the harshness of the land, now stood ominously at the heart of the village. Its stone walls seemed to glare at the approaching mob, its wooden door creaking under the weight of the cold.

"Open the door!" shouted one of the men, his voice hoarse from the freezing air.

The door opened slowly, revealing the man. He was older now, his face weathered and lined, but his eyes still held the same steely determination that had once inspired the villagers. He stood in the doorway, his frame silhouetted by the fire's dim light inside.

"What is it you want?" he asked, his voice calm but tired.

One of the women stepped forward, her face pale and gaunt. "You brought us here," she said, her voice trembling. "You promised us this Village was blessed. You told us the pooja would protect us. Why, then, are we suffering?"

Another villager chimed in, his tone accusatory. "Our children are starving! The village is more than cursed, and the ceremony no longer works. What have you done?"

The man's eyes flickered, betraying a moment of hesitation. "I have done nothing," he said, his tone unconvincing. "The land... it changes. It is beyond my control."

The crowd murmured, their frustration bubbling into anger. "Liar!" someone shouted. "You led us into this death trap! You knew this would happen!"

The man stepped out of his home, his breath fogging in the icy air. "Enough!" he bellowed, his voice cutting through the chaos. "I did not force you to come here. You came of your own will. The pooja has failed, yes, but that is no fault of mine. It is the will of the elements."

A young man from the crowd stepped forward, his eyes blazing with anger. "You've known something all along, haven't you? You've always known there was more to this land than you told us. And now, you sit in your warm home while we freeze and starve!"

The man said nothing, his silence louder than any denial.

Kumarsen interrupted the yogi, his voice filled with tension. "What did he know? Did he lie to them from the start?"

The yogi raised a hand to calm him. "Patience. What happened next is crucial."

The villagers, emboldened by the man's silence, pushed closer. "If you won't tell us the truth," said the young man, "we'll find it ourselves."

The man's face darkened, his calm demeanor cracking for the first time. "You don't understand," he said, his voice urgent. "The land... it demands balance. You cannot take without giving."

"What does that mean?" shouted a woman. "What balance? What have we given? We've only ever taken care of this land, offered it our prayers and gratitude!"

The man's eyes darted around, searching for an escape, but the crowd pressed in. "You don't understand," he repeated. "There are forces here—forces older than you or I. They are not gods. They are... watchers. They allow us to stay, but only as long as we respect the rules."

"What rules?" someone demanded. "Why didn't you tell us this before?"

The man looked away, his shoulders slumping under the weight of the truth he had carried alone for so long. "Because I thought... I thought I could protect you. I thought I could maintain the balance myself."

The crowd fell silent, the weight of his words sinking in. But the silence didn't last long.

"You've doomed us all," the young man said, his voice trembling with anger. "Whatever deal you made with this land, you've broken it. And now we're paying the price."

"I did it to save my family," the man said quietly, his voice barely audible over the wind. "To save you all."

But the crowd had already turned against him. Their fear and desperation had found a target, and their anger was unstoppable.

The yogi's voice trailed off, his expression unreadable. Kumarsen and Taran waited, their breaths caught in their throats.

"What happened to him?" Kumarsen finally asked.

The yogi shook his head. "That... is a story for another night. For now, you must understand this—whatever happened in that village, it left scars. On the people, on the land, and on the very spirit of the mountains themselves."

Kumarsen leaned forward, his voice firm. "And the curse? Is it real?"

The yogi's eyes met his, a shadow of something unspoken passing between them. "That depends on what you choose to believe. But know this—curses are not always what they seem. Sometimes, they are warnings."

The fire crackled, its embers glowing like the eyes of unseen watchers in the darkness.

***

The night began like any other—quiet, still, and cloaked in the deep silence of the mountains. But as the clock ticked toward midnight, an unnatural orange glow lit up the horizon. The cursed land, shrouded in eerie silence for generations, was ablaze.

It wasn't an ordinary fire. The flames leaped unnaturally high, consuming the ancient pine trees with a ferocity that seemed almost alive. Crackles of burning wood echoed through the valley, but what made the villagers' blood run cold were the sounds coming from the inferno.

High-pitched screeches of birds and the guttural cries of animals filled the night air, as though the very spirit of the forest was in agony. The cries were chilling, not just heard but felt, piercing through flesh and bone, leaving a deep unease in their wake.

Shivani was the first to notice. She clutched her shawl as she stood at her doorstep, her hands trembling. "Niketa!" she shouted, calling to her husband inside.

Niketa came running, his eyes widening in terror as he saw the flames licking the edges of the cursed land. "Oh, merciful Neeladri," he whispered, "this is no ordinary fire."

Soon, the village square filled with frantic villagers. Women clutched their children, men carried buckets, and the elderly muttered prayers under their breath.

"The cursed land is burning!" cried Kaalan, the local blacksmith, his voice a mix of fear and desperation. "This is a sign!"

"It's spreading fast!" shouted Harshit, pointing to the flames that now danced dangerously close to the village's outskirts.

As the villagers gathered, a new horror gripped them. A lone pine tree, standing at the boundary of the cursed land, was consumed by fire. Its branches fell with a deafening crash, sending embers flying into the first house at the edge of the village.

"The fire is here!" screamed Maya, her voice breaking as she clutched her young daughter.

People began to panic, running back to their homes to save what little they could. The crackle of flames grew louder, accompanied by the anguished cries of animals fleeing the forest.

In the midst of the chaos, Rayan, the village priest, stepped onto the temple steps. His voice boomed over the cries and whispers.

"Silence!" he commanded. "This is not the time for panic. Gather your families and come to the temple. Pray to Neeladri. Only he can save us now."

The villagers, desperate and terrified, obeyed. They crowded into the temple, their voices rising in unison as they chanted prayers.

"Neeladri, protector of these lands, save us from this fire!" Rayan intoned, leading the prayers. "Shield us with your grace!"

But outside, the fire showed no signs of abating. The flames were now mere feet from the village, their heat scorching the air. The smoke was thick, suffocating, and it seemed as though the entire mountain was under siege.

Hidden in the shadows of a nearby hill, Vettison watched the chaos unfold with cold detachment. His face, illuminated by the glow of the fire, was unreadable.

"Asuran will be pleased," he muttered.

Beside him, a hooded figure spoke in a low voice. "The fire is spreading faster than we expected. Are you sure this is wise?"

Vettison smirked. "A few burnt houses are a small price to pay for progress. The villagers will flee, and the land will be ours."

"And the insider?"

"They've done their part. For now, we wait. Let the fire do its work."

Inside the temple, the prayers reached a fever pitch. Tears streamed down the faces of the villagers as they begged Neeladri for mercy.

**Then, something extraordinary happened.**

A sudden gust of wind swept through the valley, carrying with it the faint scent of rain. The villagers looked up, their prayers faltering as they felt the first drops.

"It's raining!" a young boy shouted, his voice cutting through the tension.

But this was no ordinary rain. It came in sheets, heavy and relentless, as though the heavens themselves were pouring their fury onto the cursed land.

The villagers rushed outside, their faces turned to the sky. They watched in awe as the rain extinguished the flames with precision, sparing the village while soaking the cursed land.

Amidst the downpour, a deafening crack echoed through the valley. A bridge of fire and water appeared in the sky, stretching from the temple to the cursed land. It was a magnificent, surreal sight—flames intertwined with streams of water, moving as though guided by an unseen hand.

The villagers fell to their knees, their voices trembling as they whispered, "Neeladri..."

The fire bridge moved with purpose, dousing the flames with pinpoint accuracy. It was as though the gods themselves had descended to protect the village.

As the last ember was extinguished, the bridge dissolved into the night, leaving only the sound of the rain and the soft sobs of the villagers.

"This is a sign," Rayan declared, his voice filled with reverence. "Neeladri has saved us."

But even as the villagers celebrated their deliverance, questions lingered. Who had set the fire? And why?

On the distant hill, Vettison frowned. "This wasn't supposed to happen," he muttered.

The hooded figure beside him nodded. "The gods are watching. This will complicate things."

Vettison's eyes narrowed.

As the rain continued to fall, the villagers returned to their homes, unaware of the shadowy forces plotting against them. But the cursed land, now wet and silent, seemed to hold its own secrets, waiting for the right moment to reveal them.

The fire had changed everything. Though the flames had been extinguished, they left behind scars on the land and the villagers' hearts. Whispers of fear crept through the village's narrow lanes, growing louder with each passing day.

The cursed land was no longer just a mystery but a burden.

It was during the village meeting in the temple courtyard that the tension finally spilled over. People gathered in the temple, their faces grim and filled with worry. The murmurs of the crowd were growing louder as Rayan, the priest, stepped forward to address them.

"Rayan," called an elderly man, his voice trembling with both age and fear, "we cannot go on like this. The fire...the strange sounds...the rain. This land is cursed! Why should we keep it? Let it be someone else's problem."

The crowd roared in agreement, their fear bubbling into anger.

"Sell it!" shouted a young man from the back. "If Asuran wants it so badly, let him have it! The curse will be his to bear, not ours."

"We cannot live in fear every day," added an older woman, her hands trembling as she clutched a prayer book. "This land is bringing shame to our village. What will travelers think? They will call us cursed too!"

Rayan raised his hands, calling for silence. His calm yet commanding presence was enough to make the crowd settle.

"My friends," he began, his voice steady, "I understand your fear. But we cannot act in haste. This land is sacred. It is tied to our ancestors, to the gods themselves. Selling it to outsiders may only anger the forces we do not understand."

"Sacred?" interrupted Kaalan, the blacksmith, his voice dripping with frustration. "What sacredness has it brought us? Fire, sickness, disasters! If the gods cared, they would not let us suffer."

His words sent a ripple through the crowd.

Sukan, who was known for her sharp tongue, stepped forward. "And what if the curse isn't even real, Rayan?" she said, her eyes narrowing. "What if all these disasters are just nature, and we're clinging to old stories like fools? Let Asuran build whatever he wants—Apartments, a school, a hospital. It could even help us!"

A murmur of agreement followed her words.

But not everyone was convinced.

"Sukan," said Shivani, her voice trembling, "do you not remember the stories our grandparents told us? The land is not just cursed—it is alive. It does not forgive."

"And what do you propose we do?" retorted Sukan. "Sit here and wait for the next disaster to take our homes, our lives?"

The two women stared each other down as the tension in the crowd reached a breaking point.

Rayan raised his voice, cutting through the noise. "Enough! This village has survived for centuries because we stood united. Do not let fear divide us now. The cursed land is indeed a problem, but selling it may not be the answer."

"Then what is, Rayan?" asked Harshit, his voice heavy with exhaustion. "Tell us. Because if we do nothing, we will all suffer."

Rayan took a deep breath. "The land must be understood. Its mysteries unraveled. Only then can we decide its fate. Give me time. I will consult the scriptures, seek guidance, and find a solution."

The crowd began to disperse reluctantly, but the unease lingered. Villagers gathered in small groups, their whispers filling the air with doubt and fear.

**That Night**

Rayan sat alone in the temple, his hands clasped in prayer. The oil lamp flickered, casting dancing shadows on the walls.

"Oh, Neeladri," he whispered, "give me a sign. Show me the path. The villagers are losing faith, and I do not have the answers they seek."

As he bowed his head, a faint breeze stirred the lamp's flame. It wasn't much, but to Rayan, it felt like a gentle reassurance.

***

Meanwhile, in the dimly lit corner of a hut, a shadowy figure met with Vettison.

"You're sure they're turning against the land?" Vettison asked, his voice low and measured.

"They are terrified," said the insider, a villager whose face was obscured by the darkness. "The fire has shaken them. If you push a little harder, they'll sell."

Vettison smirked. "Good. And when they do, the cursed land will be mine. A few superstitious fools won't stop progress."

The insider hesitated. "But the fire...it wasn't natural. People are suspicious."

"Let them be," Vettison replied coldly. "Suspicion means fear. And fear makes them easy to control."

***

The next day, as the morning sun cast long golden rays across the village, Rayan once again gathered the people in the temple courtyard. The banyan tree swayed gently in the cool breeze, but the villagers' faces bore the weight of doubt and fear.

Standing at the temple steps, Rayan's voice rang out, calm yet resolute. "Brothers and sisters, I know you are worried. I know the events of recent days have left you questioning everything—the land, our traditions, even the gods themselves. But I ask you to wait."

A low murmur spread through the crowd.

"Wait?" Kaalan, the blacksmith, stepped forward, his arms crossed. "Wait for what, Rayan? More fire? More sickness? We need answers now."

Rayan raised a hand to quiet the unrest. "I understand your frustration, Kaalan. But answers are already on their way. Kumarsen is journeying to the Nandan Mountain, seeking the truth about the cursed land. He is determined to uncover its secrets—why it brings us fortune one moment and disaster the next."

The mention of Kumarsen brought a hush to the crowd.

Sukan frowned, her skepticism evident. "And what if he doesn't return, Rayan? What if there are no answers to be found? What then?"

Rayan's gaze was steady. "He will return. Kumarsen is not one to abandon his quest. His heart is strong, and his determination is greater than the challenges before him. Until then, I urge you all to trust the gods, as I have."

The older women in the crowd exchanged glances, nodding hesitantly. One of them, an elderly woman, stepped forward. "Rayan, you have always guided us well. If you believe Kumarsen will bring answers, we will wait. But how do we endure this uncertainty?"

Rayan offered her a gentle smile. "I have prayed fervently to Neeladri and the gods of our land. I have asked for their guidance, blessing upon our village, and the strength to see us through this trial. I believe the gods are with us. We must hold faith a little longer."

The crowd seemed to settle, though the undercurrent of doubt lingered.

"Faith is fine, Rayan," Kaalan said, his tone softening but still firm. "But we need a plan. What do we do if this curse takes more from us while we wait?"

"We will continue our traditions," Rayan replied. "I will lead prayers and rituals to strengthen our bond with the gods and seek their protection. And when Kumarsen returns, we will act based on the truths he uncovers."

Kaalan sighed but did not argue further. "Fine. But we cannot wait forever, Rayan. If things worsen, we will need to take action."

Rayan nodded. "I understand. But let us not forget—we are a community, bound together by trust and tradition. If we lose that, we lose more than land; we lose ourselves."

As the villagers dispersed, their steps were heavy with lingering doubt but tinged with the faintest glimmer of hope. Rayan watched them go, his heart weighed down by their trust in him.

Turning to the temple, he knelt before the sacred idol of Neeladri.

"Guide us, O Neeladri," he whispered. "Grant Kumarsen the strength to find the truth, and grant me the wisdom to lead my people through this storm."

Outside, the village waited, caught between fear of the curse and hope for Kumarsen's return.

# The Way to Yogi

The yogi's fire crackled, casting an uneasy glow on Kumarsen and Taran as they leaned closer. The shadows flickered ominously, as if the forest itself were listening.

"This," said the yogi in a voice that trembled like the firelight, "is where the true horror began. The moment the first settler revealed the truth, the villagers understood why their lives had spiraled into despair."

The snowstorm had grown fiercer, howling against the walls of the man's home. The villagers, crammed into his small house, demanded answers. Their faces, pale with cold and fear, were illuminated by the dim light of an oil lamp. The old man, seated near the hearth, looked as though he carried the weight of a hundred lifetimes. His hands trembled as he held them near the fire, his eyes staring into the flames as if searching for courage.

"I didn't set out to bring this upon us," the old man began, his eyes avoiding those of the crowd. "When I came here with my family, the land was barren, and survival was near impossible. For two days, I poured my heart into prayers, calling upon the gods for their blessings. I performed every ritual I knew, worshipping Agni, Jal, Vayu, Prithvi, and Akasha. But nothing happened."

A murmur rippled through the crowd.

"You said the gods blessed this land!" shouted a young man, his voice edged with accusation. "That's why my father and I settled here!"

The old man shook his head slowly, his frail frame trembling. "That's the lie I told you all to protect the truth. On the second night, exhausted and defeated, I fell asleep during the ritual. In my dream, a figure appeared. Not a god, not a saint, but something... else."

His voice dropped to a whisper. "He was cloaked in darkness, with eyes like burning coals. He told me that the gods had abandoned this place because it wasn't meant for man. But he—this being—could make it a paradise. All he wanted was devotion. A temple built in his honor."

The villagers gasped, their shock palpable.

"Why didn't you tell anyone?" an elderly woman demanded, her wrinkled hands trembling as she clutched her shawl. "Why didn't you let us choose?"

"Because I didn't think I'd have to," the old man admitted, his voice filled with regret. "He promised me prosperity, health, and peace for generations. And he delivered. Crops flourished, families grew strong, and the land became everything we needed it to be. I thought we could live quietly, honoring his request when the time was right."

"Then why is everything falling apart now?" a burly farmer asked. "Why has he taken back his blessing?"

The old man sighed deeply, his shoulders slumping under the weight of his guilt. "Because I failed him. He wanted a temple, a place where his name would be remembered and his power honored. I promised him we would build it. But years turned into decades, and I kept putting it off, telling myself there was time. Now, he's angry. He's withdrawn his power as a warning."

"What does he want now?" someone whispered fearfully.

"To remind us of our debt," the old man replied gravely.

A young woman stepped forward, her face pale but determined. "You said you performed the rituals for two days. Are you telling us you didn't actually complete the prayers to the gods? That all this time, our prosperity came from some... devil?"

The old man met her gaze, his eyes filled with remorse. "Yes. I prayed to the gods, but when they didn't answer, I turned to him in my dream. I thought I had no choice. The ritual to the gods never brought us prosperity. It was his power that did."

The crowd erupted in murmurs, anger and fear swirling together.

"We've been living a lie!" someone shouted.

"How do we fix this?" another voice demanded.

The old man raised a trembling hand for silence. "There's only one way. We must fulfill the promise I made all those years ago. We must build the temple."

Silence fell over the room, broken only by the crackle of the fire.

A young man named Narayan, his face set with determination, stepped forward. "And if we don't? What happens then?"

The old man's eyes darkened, his voice dropping to a whisper. "If we don't honor the pact, he will take back everything. The crops, the health of our families, the very land we stand on. He will turn it into a wasteland."

The villagers looked at one another, their faces etched with fear and uncertainty.

"But what if he's lying?" the burly farmer asked, his voice trembling. "What if this so-called devil only wants to destroy us in the end?"

The old man shook his head. "I've seen his power. He can give, and he can take away. We've already broken our promise. Now, we must decide if we're willing to risk his wrath further."

The crowd fell silent, each person lost in their thoughts. Finally, a young woman spoke up. "If we build this temple, won't we be tied to him forever? Is that the kind of life we want for ourselves and our children?"

The old man's eyes filled with tears. "I don't know. But I do know that we've already accepted his gifts. And now, he's calling in his debt."

The villagers turned to one another, their fear and anger giving way to a heavy, suffocating uncertainty. The decision before them was no longer just about their survival. It was about their souls.

"Then we have to choose," Narayan said, his voice steady. "Do we honor this pact and live under his shadow, or do we fight to reclaim our lives, no matter the cost?"

The old man looked at him, his face lined with regret. "The choice is yours now. But know this—there is no path without consequences."

The villagers stared at one another, the weight of their choice pressing down on them like the darkness outside. In the distance, the wind howled, as if echoing the devil's impatience.

***

The village was steeped in tension, its once harmonious community now fractured by fear and desperation. In the weeks following the old man's revelation, heated arguments erupted daily in the village. The villagers were torn—some argued for honoring the pact with the dark force to bring back prosperity, while others, horrified by the truth, insisted on severing all ties with the devil and the man who had bound them to him.

"He lied to us from the beginning!" shouted Narayan, his voice echoing through the gathering. "We've built our lives on falsehoods. If we build that temple, we'll be chaining ourselves to this darkness forever!"

"And what's your solution, Narayan?" countered an elderly farmer. "Watch our children starve? Let the land die? We've already accepted his gifts. Denying him now will only make things worse!"

"He's already taken back his so-called blessings!" a woman cried out, holding up a bundle of shriveled roots. "The crops are gone, the river's frozen, and we can't even light fires to keep warm! Are we going to let this devil destroy us completely?"

The old man stood silently at the edge of the crowd, his weathered face a mask of guilt and sorrow. His family huddled behind him, their eyes downcast. His son, a man in his forties, finally stepped forward, his voice trembling with emotion.

"We never wanted this for the village," he said. "My father thought he was saving us all. But if you want to punish someone, punish him—not us. We've worked as hard as any of you to keep this village alive."

"Your family brought this curse upon us!" a young man shouted, pointing an accusatory finger. "You should all leave! Maybe then the devil will take his wrath with you!"

The crowd murmured in agreement, their anger and fear boiling over.

Over the weeks, the arguments grew more heated, turning into threats. The villagers stopped speaking to the old man and his family except to hurl insults or blame. Children were warned not to go near their houses. The family's isolation deepened, their shame palpable.

As the winter months dragged on, the situation grew dire. The river remained frozen solid, its waters inaccessible. The forest, damp from relentless snow, yielded wood too wet to burn. Hunger gnawed at the villagers, and the cold seeped into their bones. Desperation turned into fury.

One freezing evening, the village council summoned the old man to the temple square. Snow swirled around the gathering, the villagers bundled in layers against the biting cold.

The council leader, a stout man with a heavy brow, stepped forward. "We've deliberated long enough," he announced, his voice cutting through the icy air. "You and your family have brought this upon us. Your pact with the devil has cursed this village, and now we all suffer because of it."

The old man looked up, his eyes hollow. "I tried to save us," he said weakly. "I didn't know it would come to this. If we build the temple, the darkness will lift—"

"We will not build a temple to a devil!" Narayan interrupted, his voice ringing with conviction. "We would rather struggle and find our way back to the light than bow to darkness. You've had your say, and we've made our choice."

The council leader raised his hand for silence. "Your actions have left us no choice. You and your family must leave this village. Perhaps your absence will lift this curse."

A gasp rippled through the crowd, followed by murmurs of agreement.

The old man's son stepped forward, his face flushed with anger. "You're throwing us out? After everything we've done for this village?"

"You've done enough," a woman snapped. "Leave before more harm comes to us."

The old man's shoulders slumped, his frail frame bending under the weight of his guilt. He looked out over the crowd, searching for any sign of compassion, but found only hardened faces.

Finally, he nodded. "If my leaving will bring peace, then so be it."

His voice broke as he added, "But remember this—you chose to turn your backs on the only power that could save this land. I hope your gods hear your cries because the devil won't."

The villagers watched in silence as the old man turned and walked away, his family trailing behind him. The snow fell heavier, shrouding them as they disappeared into the dark forest.

The council leader turned to the crowd. "It's done. The old man will have to leave."

The villagers stood in uneasy silence, the weight of their decision pressing down on them like the snow-laden sky. They had driven out the man who had built their village, but whether they had also driven out the darkness remained to be seen.

Kumarsen and Taran sat in stunned silence, the cold mountain air around them feeling heavier as the Yogi continued his tale. The flickering light of the small fire they had built danced on the Yogi's face, casting sharp shadows that made his expressions seem even more intense.

Taran, his voice barely above a whisper, asked, "What happened to the family after they left the village?"

The Yogi took a deep breath, his eyes distant as though peering into the past. "They were broken—outcast by their own people. The man, his wife, and their two children walked away from the only home they'd ever known, clutching what little they could carry. Their hearts were heavy, and the winter's chill bit at their resolve."

He paused, his voice dropping lower, pulling Kumarsen and Taran deeper into the unfolding story.

The man and his family wandered the snowy paths aimlessly, their once proud faces shadowed with despair. As night began to fall, the biting cold forced them to make a decision.

"We'll stay on the farm," the man declared, his voice firm despite the weariness in his tone. "The villagers may not want us, but the land is still ours."

His wife, though hesitant, nodded in agreement. "If we're careful, they won't see us. We can rest there for tonight."

The family trudged through the darkness, their feet crunching the snow-laden fields until they reached a small, secluded hut in the middle of the farm. It was a modest shelter, typically used to store tools and house two bulls. The animals stirred as they entered, but the family's gentle whispers soon calmed them.

The wife lit a small oil lamp, its dim glow offering the only comfort in the cold, desolate night. She spread blankets on the floor for the children, who quickly curled up and fell into an uneasy sleep. The man sat silently in the corner, his gaze fixed on the far wall as though lost in thought.

Hours passed, and the wife, too, succumbed to sleep. But the man's restlessness grew. The weight of his guilt and the burden of his choices pressed down on him like the snow outside. Unable to bear it any longer, he rose quietly, careful not to wake his family, and stepped out into the freezing night.

The farm stretched out before him, a ghostly white expanse under the pale light of the crescent moon. He made his way to the edge of the field, where a small pile of stones lay, covered in frost.

He knelt before it, his hands trembling as he scraped away the snow to reveal the largest stone at the center. It was smooth and dark, glinting faintly in the moonlight.

With a deep breath, he gathered dried twigs and straw, building a small fire around the stone. The flames licked upward, their warmth barely reaching him in the frigid air.

Inside the hut, his wife stirred. She opened her eyes and immediately noticed her husband's absence. Alarmed, she wrapped a shawl around herself and stepped outside, where the faint glow of the fire caught her eye.

"why?" she called softly, her voice tinged with worry.

She approached cautiously, the sight before her stopping her in her tracks. Her husband knelt before the fire, his hands clasped in fervent prayer as he muttered incomprehensible words to the stone.

"What are you doing?" she demanded, her voice sharp as she stepped closer.

The man didn't turn. His voice, low and resolute, carried through the cold night. "I'm praying. I'm asking for forgiveness... and for help."

"Forgiveness? Help?" she repeated, her tone rising. "From that thing?" She pointed at the stone, her disbelief turning to anger. "You're worshiping it again? After everything that's happened? After we were thrown out of the village because of this?"

He finally turned to her, his face illuminated by the fire. "What choice do we have?" he said, his voice steady despite the desperation in his eyes. "The villagers won't take us back. The gods have turned their faces from us. This is the only power that has ever helped us."

"We don't need help from that... that *thing!*" she snapped, her anger giving way to frustration. "We have some money saved. We can leave this place, start over in another village—or even in the city!"

The man shook his head slowly, his expression resolute. "You don't understand," he said. "It's not about starting over. It's about survival. If we leave, it won't let us go. This land... it binds us to it. We owe it a debt."

His wife stared at him, horrified. "You're talking nonsense," she said, her voice trembling. "We're not bound to anything. We're leaving tomorrow. We'll take the children and whatever we can carry and we'll go—far away from this cursed place."

The man looked back at the stone, his shoulders sagging under the weight of her words. "You can go," he said quietly. "But I can't. I made a promise. If I leave, it will follow us. It will find us, no matter where we go. This is the only way to protect you... to protect them."

His wife took a step back, her breath catching in her throat. She turned and hurried back to the hut, her mind racing with fear and confusion.

The Yogi paused, his voice heavy with foreboding. Kumarsen and Taran leaned forward, their faces pale in the flickering firelight.

"What happened next?" Taran asked, his voice barely audible.

The air grew colder around the small hut as the night deepened, the silence outside broken only by the occasional rustle of leaves and the heavy breathing of the restless bulls. Inside, the man's wife and children huddled together for warmth, their expressions etched with exhaustion and despair.

Meanwhile, outside, the man knelt before the fire he had ignited in the middle of his farm. The flames danced wildly, casting eerie, flickering shadows across his gaunt face. He held the black stone tightly in his hands, its surface oddly cold despite the proximity to the fire. His murmurs filled the air, a mix of chants and whispers in a language that didn't belong to the world of the living.

His wife peeked out from the hut, her voice trembling with anger and fear.

"Why are you doing this?" she demanded, stepping closer, her hands clutching her shawl tightly. "We've already lost everything—our home, our standing, our respect. This...this won't bring it back."

The man didn't turn to face her. His eyes were fixed on the stone, his voice unwavering.

"I'll bring us back," he said hoarsely. "I'll bring back what we've lost. They will see my power, my devotion. They'll beg for forgiveness."

She knelt beside him, tears brimming in her eyes as she grabbed his arm. "We don't need their forgiveness!" she cried. "We have money. We can leave this cursed place and start fresh. In a new village, a new city. Somewhere far from this madness."

He wrenched his arm free, his gaze as unyielding as the mountain itself. "This land is ours," he said, his voice cold. "I built everything here. I won't let them take it away. And I won't let the darkness consume me without fighting back. The Devil blessed us once—he will do so again."

His wife recoiled at his words, her face pale in the firelight. "Do you hear yourself? You're calling for *him* again! The same darkness that brought us here!" She pointed at the stone. "That thing—whatever it is—it's not going to save us. It will destroy us!"

The man ignored her protests, his chants growing louder, more insistent. The fire rose higher, the heat licking at the night air with an unnatural ferocity. His voice reached a fever pitch as he placed the stone at the heart of the flames.

Suddenly, the wind picked up, fierce and howling, swirling around the farm like an invisible force had awakened. The bulls in the nearby stable snorted nervously, their hooves stamping against the ground. His wife stumbled back, shielding her face from the wind.

And then, it happened.

The fire twisted into a towering column of light, its core shifting and rippling until it no longer looked like fire at all. From the center of the inferno, a form began to take shape—tall, slender, and translucent, yet unmistakably menacing.

The figure stepped forward, its features a blend of shadow and glass, constantly shifting and impossible to define. It loomed over the kneeling man, radiating a chilling presence that seemed to drain the very warmth from the air.

His wife gasped, covering her mouth in terror. "What...what is that?"

The man, shaking but resolute, raised his hands in reverence. "You came," he whispered, his voice trembling. "I knew you would come."

The translucent figure tilted its head, a voice like the echo of thunder rumbling through the air.

The scene froze in that moment, the fire still roaring, the air electric with tension. The man's wife stumbled back toward the hut, clutching her children tightly as she whispered, "What has he done?"

The figure's form shimmered, its gaze fixed on the man who had summoned it. The night seemed to hold its breath as the Devil asked him the "**Question**".

The translucent figure loomed over the man, its shimmering form flickering like a flame caught in a storm. Its voice, deep and resonant, reverberated through the cold night air, freezing the very breath in the man's lungs.

"Where is my temple?" the Devil demanded, its eyes—dark, yet glimmering with an otherworldly light—boring into him.

The man trembled, his hands clasped together in supplication. The wind around them swirled wildly, bending the nearby trees as if bowing to the presence of the unholy being.

"My Lord," the man stammered, barely able to form the words. "I...I tried. I wanted to build it. But the villagers—"

The figure cut him off, taking a step closer. Its translucent form radiated a freezing energy that made the fire beside them sputter and hiss. "*Tried?*" it hissed, the word sharp as a blade. "Do not speak of trying, mortal. It was your promise. Your oath. And yet I see no temple standing here."

The man's wife, peeking through the small hut's opening, watched in terrified silence, clutching her children tightly. Even the bulls had gone eerily still, as though sensing the presence of something unnatural and far beyond their understanding.

The man bowed his head lower, his voice breaking. "Forgive me, my Lord. Please. I... I failed you. The villagers turned against me. They no longer worship you. They cast me out, abandoned me. I—I had no power to fulfill my promise."

The Devil leaned closer, its towering form now inches from the man. Its voice grew colder, quieter, but with a venom that made the man's skin crawl.

"You dare speak of failure? You dare speak of abandonment? Who was it that gave you life when your family faced death? Who filled these lands with prosperity and abundance, so you could build your pathetic village? Who demanded so little in return—a temple, a symbol of gratitude—and you denied me even that?"

The man shuddered under the weight of those words, tears streaming down his face. "You saved us," he admitted, his voice barely audible. "You gave us everything. And I betrayed you."

The Devil straightened, its form pulsing with an ominous energy. The flames around the stone surged higher, burning an unnatural blue. "And yet you still dare to summon me," it said, each word dripping with disdain. "Why? What could a failure like you possibly want from me now?"

The man fell prostrate on the frozen ground, his voice cracking as he pleaded. "Please, my Lord! Save us once more! The land is cursed again. The crops fail, the rivers freeze, and the village is dying. Give me one more chance—I beg you!"

The Devil's laughter rumbled through the air like distant thunder, harsh and mocking. "One more chance?" it said, circling the man. "You squandered decades, mortal. You and your village grew fat on the blessings I gave you. And now, when the price is due, you think to bargain with me?"

The man raised his head, desperation etched into every line of his face. "I can fix this! I've built a small temple on this land—it's modest, but it's something. If you restore the land, and bring prosperity again, I swear to build you the grand temple you deserve. I'll dedicate the rest of my life to it. I'll ensure the villagers worship you again!"

The Devil stopped, its form flickering as though considering the words. Then, with a sudden, furious burst of energy, it slammed its hand down, sending a shockwave through the ground. The fire roared higher, casting grotesque shadows on the surrounding trees.

"You insult me," the Devil growled, its voice now a cacophony of rage. "A *small* temple? After fifty years of lies and broken promises, you offer me scraps? You dare reduce me to this?"

The man recoiled, his forehead pressed against the earth. "I'm sorry! Please—have mercy!"

The Devil's form grew darker, more defined, as it loomed closer, its anger palpable. "Mercy?" it spat. "You will learn what mercy is, mortal. But not tonight."

The scene hung heavy with tension, the firelight painting the Devil's wrath across the trembling man's face. The air itself seemed to hold its breath, awaiting the next move.

The man knelt on the frozen ground, his forehead pressed so low it nearly touched the dirt. His body trembled with every word he uttered. "Please, my Lord! Give me another chance. I will do anything. Anything! I beg you. Spare my family, spare the village!"

The translucent figure loomed over him, its form rippling like a flame caught in an unseen wind. Its eyes, glowing with a malevolent light, narrowed in disdain. "Another chance?" the Devil snarled, its voice like a jagged whisper slicing through the frigid air. "I gave you decades. Decades to fulfill your promise. And all I see is failure!"

The man's wife, standing just inside the hut, gasped as the icy wind tore through the air, her eyes wide with fear as she watched the horrifying scene unfold.

The Devil's form shifted, growing darker, its edges flickering violently. "Do you think your pathetic pleas will move me?" it said, its voice echoing as though it came from the depths of the earth. "I have come to understand one thing, mortal: *You* are incapable of keeping your word."

The man raised his head slightly, his face pale and soaked with tears. "No, my Lord! I will prove myself! Just give me the strength, the chance to—"

"Enough!" the Devil roared, the sound reverberating through the night. The ground beneath the man shook, and the fire around the stone exploded into a column of blue flame, throwing grotesque shadows across the farm.

The Devil leaned closer, its translucent form now mere inches from the man. "You have wasted my time, my gifts, my patience," it hissed. "And now, I will take matters into my own hands."

Before the man could respond, the Devil straightened, its form expanding and darkening until it blotted out the flickering firelight. "You wanted my help? Then I will give it. But no longer as an outsider watching over this land."

The man's breath caught in his throat as the Devil's form began to convulse and shift, its edges curling inward like smoke being drawn into a single point. The air crackled with an unholy energy, and the light from the fire dimmed as if even the flames feared what was happening.

"No!" the man cried, his voice cracking. "What are you doing?"

The Devil's voice boomed, now coming from everywhere and nowhere. "I will no longer wait for your pathetic worship or promises. I will take control myself!"

And with that, the Devil's translucent form lunged toward the man. A horrifying light—both blinding and dark at once—burst forth as the Devil's essence poured into the man's body.

The man screamed, his voice twisted into something unrecognizable, a mixture of pain, fear, and something far darker. His body convulsed violently as the Devil merged with him, his eyes glowing a fiery orange. His veins pulsed with an unnatural black light, and his shadow twisted and writhed like it had a life of its own.

The man's wife screamed, clutching her children tighter. "No! Stop this! Please!"

Her words were drowned out by the sound of the Devil's laughter, now coming from the man's mouth but layered with its own echo. The man—no longer himself—stood slowly, his movements jerky and unnatural. His eyes burned with an otherworldly fire, and his voice came out in a low, guttural tone.

"I am here now," the possessed man said, his voice reverberating like thunder. "This land, this village, this mountain—it will all bow to me."

The wife's instincts took over. "Run!" she shouted to her children, pulling them from the hut. The bulls, as if sensing the dark power, broke free from their chains with frenzied strength and bolted into the jungle, their hooves pounding against the frozen ground.

The wife glanced back only once, tears streaming down her face as she saw the terrifying figure of her husband—or what was left of him—standing in the middle of the blazing blue fire. The darkness around him seemed to pulse and grow, reaching out like living tendrils.

She turned and ran toward the village, clutching her children, her heart pounding with terror. Behind her, the unnatural laughter of the Devil echoed through the night, a haunting sound that promised doom to all who heard it.

The farm was now a place of nightmares, swallowed by a darkness that no one would dare to face.

The icy wind carried the panicked cries of the woman as she stumbled into the heart of the village, her children clutching her torn shawl. Her voice cracked with desperation as she shouted, "The Devil has taken him! He's building a temple for it—stones bigger than any man could lift!"

Villagers emerged from their huts, lanterns in hand, their faces pale with fear and disbelief. An uneasy murmur spread among them, growing louder with each second.

"What is she saying?"
"A temple for the Devil?"
"Where is her husband?"

The village elder raised his hand to quiet the commotion. His voice, though shaky, held authority. "Speak clearly, woman. What has happened?"

She clutched her chest, gasping for air. "He… he's possessed. The Devil entered him. I saw it with my own eyes! He was standing in flames, speaking in a voice that wasn't his. Now, he's at the river, lifting stones no human could lift. He's building that cursed temple!"

The elder's face darkened. "What madness have we brought upon ourselves?"

From the ridge at the edge of the village, a young boy called out, "Look!"

The villagers rushed to the top of the hill, their feet crunching on the snow-covered ground. From there, they could see the river glinting in the moonlight—and the figure of the possessed man.

The sight chilled them to their cores.

The man—if it could still be called that—moved with unnatural strength, hoisting boulders the size of oxen as though they were mere pebbles. His movements were mechanical, inhuman, and his glowing eyes pierced through the darkness. Around him, the air shimmered with an eerie glow, and a faint sound, like whispered chants, drifted up the hill.

A young woman gasped, clutching her husband's arm. "What kind of power is this?"

The elder shook his head, his voice heavy with despair. "No man should have this strength. It is the Devil's doing."

"What do we do now?" a farmer asked, his voice trembling. "We can't fight this… thing. It's not human anymore."

The wife of the possessed man stepped forward, her voice quivering but resolute. "We must pray. Pray to the only power that can save us. Neel Mountain. It has stood as our guardian for generations. If it cannot help us, no one can."

The villagers exchanged uneasy glances. Neel Mountain, towering above the village with its snow-covered peaks, had always been a source of reverence and fear. Its name, derived from its icy blue hue in the heart of winter, carried an air of mysticism.

The elder nodded gravely. "Then we shall pray."

The villagers gathered at the top of the ridge, where they could see the mountain in its full majesty, bathed in the silver glow of the moon. The elder raised his hands, his voice trembling as he began the prayer.

"Oh, Neel Mountain, guardian of our land, we call upon you in our time of need. A great evil has been summoned upon your sacred soil. We beg you, protect us from this darkness. Save our village from destruction."

The villagers, kneeling on the frozen ground, joined in unison, their voices rising in a desperate plea. "Neel Mountain, save us!"

As their prayers echoed into the night, a cold wind swept through the valley, carrying with it a strange, almost electric energy. The villagers fell silent, their eyes fixed on the mountain as if expecting it to answer.

The elder whispered, "If Neel Mountain hears us, we will see a sign."

From the direction of the river, the possessed man's voice boomed, louder than thunder, cutting through the stillness. "Pray all you want! No mountain can save you now. This land belongs to me!"

But even as he spoke, the villagers noticed something. The snow on Neel Mountain's peak began to glow faintly, a soft blue light that grew brighter with each passing second. The villagers gasped, their prayers growing louder.

The elder's voice broke with emotion. "It is listening. Neel Mountain is listening!"

Below, the possessed man paused, his glowing eyes narrowing as he turned toward the mountain. For a moment, the chanting whispers around him seemed to falter, replaced by an ominous silence.

The villagers held their breath, their eyes darting between the mountain and the figure by the river. The fate of their village—and perhaps their lives—now hung in the balance.

***

## Neeladri of the Neel Parvat

The snow on Neel Mountain glowed brighter, pulsating like a heartbeat. The villagers, huddled on the ridge, shielded their eyes as the light intensified, illuminating the entire valley in a surreal azure hue. The air turned icy, yet it carried an undeniable energy, humming with power.

"Do you see that?" whispered one of the elders, his voice trembling.

The elder nodded solemnly. "It is Neeladri. He is here."

From the glowing peak of Neel Mountain, a sudden gust of wind erupted, swirling snow and ice into a spiraling vortex. The villagers gasped as the winds howled louder, resonating with a deep, thunderous tone that seemed to emanate from the heart of the mountain itself.

Then, from within the vortex, a figure emerged—a towering, radiant being of ice and light. His form was both human and celestial, with skin like translucent crystal, reflecting the shimmering blues and whites of the mountain. His eyes burned with an intense silver fire, piercing through the darkness like twin stars.

**Neeladri Dev had arrived.**

He descended gracefully, stepping as if the air itself bowed beneath his feet. Each step sent ripples of frost across the ground, freezing even the flowing river below. The villagers watched in awe and terror as he moved closer, his massive figure both ethereal and overwhelmingly present.

As Neeladri reached the edge of the village, his voice boomed across the valley, deeper than the earth and sharper than the winter wind. It was not a voice that could be ignored.

**"Who dares defile my sacred land?"**

The villagers fell to their knees, their faces pressed to the frozen ground. None dared to speak. The aura of power surrounding Neeladri was overwhelming, suffocating even, as though the mountain itself had risen to judge them.

At the riverbank, the possessed man froze, his glowing eyes narrowing as he turned to face the deity. The translucent figure of the Devil within him flickered, and for a moment, the villagers could see both forms—the man and the shadowy entity controlling him.

The Devil's voice, oily and deep, slithered through the air. "Ah, Neeladri. It's been centuries since you've graced this land with your presence."

Neeladri's fiery eyes locked onto the possessed man. His expression was a mix of divine wrath and unyielding resolve. "You dare to corrupt this place with your foul presence? Your darkness has no claim here!"

The Devil chuckled mockingly, the sound echoing unnaturally. "This land was nothing until I gave it purpose. I fed your people, Neeladri. I made this village thrive when you remained silent."

"You fed them lies!" Neeladri's voice shook the ground, cracks forming in the frozen earth beneath his feet. "You lured them with false prosperity, chaining their souls to your darkness. Your greed has poisoned this land, and I will not stand for it."

The translucent figure within the man laughed again, but this time it was strained. The light radiating from Neeladri grew stronger, and the Devil's form flickered like a flame caught in a gale.

The villagers dared to lift their heads slightly, witnessing the confrontation with wide, disbelieving eyes. One of them whispered, "He's… he's driving the Devil back."

Neeladri raised a hand, and from his palm, a beam of icy light shot forth, striking the ground near the man. The Devil roared in pain, the sound reverberating like an avalanche.

The man, still possessed, dropped the massive boulder he had been holding. It shattered into shards of ice as he stumbled backward, his body convulsing. The Devil's translucent form began to crack under the pressure of Neeladri's power.

"You will leave this land," Neeladri commanded, his voice like a thousand crashing glaciers. "And you will never return."

But the Devil, though weakened, was defiant. "If I must leave, then I will take this temple with me. Let them suffer in darkness without my gifts."

Neeladri's eyes burned brighter, his expression hardening. "Enough of your lies. This land needs neither your gifts nor your corruption. It will heal, as it always has, under the protection of its true guardian."

Neeladri raised both hands, and the glowing light surrounding him exploded outward in a blinding flash. The villagers cried out, shielding their eyes as the ground shook violently.

Opposite him, the Devil still wore the man's body, though his energy flickered weakly, like a dying ember. Yet his voice carried venom and defiance as he spoke.

'If not I, Neeladri, who will save this mountain from its fate?' the Devil spat, his voice resonating like an echo in the hollow valley. 'Tell your precious villagers the truth. You see the future as clearly as I do. Their descendants will abandon this land. Their homes will crumble, their fields will go barren, and their stories will fade. They will leave, Neeladri, and outsiders will come. They will trample over your sacred soil, cutting roads through forests and rivers. They will destroy what I cannot.'

Neeladri's silver eyes burned brighter, the glow reflecting the rage of a thousand winters. Yet his voice was calm, like the steady flow of a river. 'You speak of truths, Devil, but your words are twisted. The land's spirit is eternal, even if its caretakers change. You offer fear, despair, and chaos. I offer hope and redemption.'

The man laughed, a hollow sound that sent shivers down the spines of the villagers watching from afar. 'Hope? Redemption?' he mocked. 'You think those will sustain them when the winters grow colder, when the crops fail, when their children leave for cities they cannot resist? You think your light will hold them here when the comforts of the world beyond call them away? You may defeat me here today, Neeladri, but you cannot defeat time. You cannot hold their devotion forever.'

Neeladri stepped forward, his luminous aura growing, casting long shadows that seemed to swallow the Devil's form. 'I do not need to hold them, Devil. The land itself will call to them. It will sing to their hearts, even if it takes generations. Those who leave will carry its spirit with them. Those who return will find it waiting. The mountains are not mine to control—they are alive, eternal. They belong to those who choose to honor them.'

The Devil recoiled, the light of Neeladri's truth striking him like a physical blow. But he wasn't done. Summoning his remaining strength, he sneered, 'And what of the present? Will you give them happiness, Neeladri? Will you shield them from the pain of loss and the burden of hardship? You may win this battle, but you cannot change their fate.'

Neeladri raised his hand, and the winds howled through the valley, carrying his voice like thunder. 'Their happiness is not mine to give, Devil. It is theirs to find, in the soil they till, in the rivers they drink from, in the love they share. I offer them the strength to endure, to persevere, and to protect what matters. That is the legacy of Mountains.'

The Devil snarled, his energy faltering as Neeladri's power bore down upon him. With a final surge of defiance, he roared, 'You think you've silenced me, Neeladri? You think you've won? I am patient, and I am eternal. I will wait, as I always have. And when they falter—and they will—I will be there to offer them what you cannot.'

Neeladri raised his other hand, and a wave of light burst forth, striking the Devil with the force of an avalanche. The possessed man collapsed to the ground, his body trembling as the Devil's translucent soul was forced out. The villagers gasped as the dark, flickering essence of the Devil hovered above the temple's foundation.

The Devil's voice grew faint but venomous. 'This land...this land...will bear my mark. Though incomplete, it will remain. No one will dare use it for generations. But I will wait. I will always wait.'

With that, the Devil's form began to dissolve, scattering like ashes on the wind. His presence seeped into the soil, the very ground where the temple stones lay. A deep, eerie silence followed, broken only by the distant cry of an eagle circling above.

The villagers stood frozen, unable to move or speak.

The wind carried an eerie stillness as the translucent Devil dissipated into the soil, his venomous promise lingering like a shadow over the land. The possessed man, now free, lay motionless on the cold earth. His chest rose and fell with shallow breaths, his body frail from the ordeal. Neeladri stood tall above him, his radiant form glowing with the light of the mountains and rivers, his presence both overwhelming and calming.

The villagers watched from afar, trembling in awe and fear, their hands clutched together in silent prayers.

With a motion as fluid as the flowing rivers, Neeladri bent down and placed his hand on the man's shoulder. The touch was both gentle and commanding, like the weight of a snow-laden branch ready to fall. The man stirred, his eyes fluttering open. For a moment, they met Neeladri's piercing gaze, and tears welled in his eyes—not of fear, but of remorse.

"You are free from the Devil's grasp," Neeladri said, his voice echoing like a deep canyon. "But you bear the burden of your choices. Look around you. The land cries out for honor, for protection. The villagers trusted you, and you faltered. Now, you must rise—not as a man seeking power, but as one who protects what matters."

The man's voice trembled as he whispered, "I...I failed. I brought darkness to this land. How can I undo what has been done?"

Neeladri's eyes softened, but his voice held firm authority. "You will not undo the past. But you will shape the future. Tell your people this: prosperity belongs to those who honor the land, who choose to protect its spirit. Build no temple to greed or fear. Instead, once a year, gather as one to honor this land's true protectors. Speak to me, and I will listen. **For I will come to you and your descendants, and I will guide you when the time is right.**"

The villagers, hearing Neeladri's words, began to kneel one by one, their hearts heavy with guilt and gratitude. The land beneath their feet seemed to stir, the air warmer, the frost melting in droplets that shimmered in the moonlight.

The man, tears streaming down his face, bowed low before Neeladri. "I will. I swear on my life and my bloodline, we will honor you, Neeladri. And this land...this sacred land will be our bond to you."

Neeladri straightened, his towering form glowing brighter. His gaze turned to the incomplete temple behind them. The stones piled high seemed to vibrate, their edges illuminated by a golden light.

"This land bears the Devil's curse," Neeladri declared, his voice shaking the earth. "For centuries, it will remain barren, a scar upon the mountain. No crop will grow here, no structure will stand. But let it serve as a reminder—to falter is human, but to rise again is divine."

With a sweep of his hand, the air erupted in a brilliant cascade of light. The villagers shielded their eyes as the incomplete temple began to crumble. The stones cracked, splitting apart as though struck by an invisible force. A low rumble echoed through the valley as the entire structure collapsed into dust, the soil swallowing the remains until nothing was left but an empty, silent expanse.

Neeladri turned to the villagers, his voice softening. "Remember this day. Pass down this tale to your children, and their children after them. Honor the land, and it will honor you in return."

With those words, his form began to dissolve into the wind, his luminous presence fading like the first light of dawn. His final words lingered on the air, a promise and a warning.

"Prosperity is not in temples or treasures. It is in the hearts of those who protect what is sacred."

The villagers stood in silence, their gazes fixed on the spot where Neeladri had vanished. The man knelt on the soil, clutching the earth with trembling hands. His wife and children approached him, their eyes filled with both relief and sorrow.

The wind carried a faint, melodic hum, as if the mountain itself was singing a lullaby. And in that moment, the villagers knew their land had been saved—but the responsibility of its future rested in their hands.

Kumarsen and Taran exchanged a glance, their thoughts racing.

'Do you think...' Taran began, his voice barely above a whisper, 'that the Devil's curse still lingers?'

The yogi gazed into the fire, his expression unreadable. 'Perhaps. But curses are powerless if the heart of the people remains strong. The question is not whether the Devil waits. It is whether you will rise to honor the land that bore you.'

The flames crackled, their light casting shifting shadows on the cave walls. At that moment, the weight of the mountains seemed to press down on Kumarsen and Taran, as if asking them the same question.

# The Protector of the Mountain

The journey back to the village was swift compared to their arduous climb to the Nandan Mountains. The crisp mountain air seemed lighter now, the burden of mystery less oppressive but not entirely gone. Kumarsen and Taran carried the weight of what they had learned from the yogi—the truth about the cursed land, the bargain struck generations ago, and the delicate balance between human ambition and the mountains' natural order.

As the sun dipped behind the peaks, painting the sky in fiery hues, the two men trudged onward. Exhaustion weighed heavily on them, and when they reached a small clearing near a stream, they decided to rest. Taran spread out his shawl on the ground, while Kumarsen leaned against a sturdy pine tree.

"We'll move as soon as the stars come out," Taran muttered, his voice heavy with weariness.

But Kumarsen's eyelids were already drooping, and before long, he succumbed to sleep.

In his dream, the forest was alive with a strange, ethereal glow. Shadows danced between the trees as if the moonlight itself had taken form. Kumarsen found himself standing on a narrow trail that wound deep into the jungle.

From the corner of his eye, he saw a figure—tall, majestic, and shrouded in a bluish aura. It was unmistakably Neeladri. The demigod moved with grace, his presence commanding yet unearthly. Without thinking, Kumarsen began to follow him.

"Wait!" Kumarsen called out, but Neeladri didn't stop. His form glided effortlessly through the dense forest, slipping between the trees like mist. Kumarsen stumbled over roots and rocks, struggling to keep up.

The jungle grew darker, the trees towering like silent sentinels. Strange whispers filled the air, not from Neeladri but from the forest itself, as if the land were alive and murmuring secrets. The path grew narrower, almost suffocating, but Kumarsen pressed on. He couldn't lose sight of Neeladri.

Finally, the demigod paused in a small clearing bathed in silver light. Kumarsen approached cautiously, his heart pounding. But as he reached out to speak, Neeladri vanished. The clearing fell into an eerie silence.

"Neeladri!" Kumarsen shouted, spinning around, searching for any sign of the demigod. The shadows seemed to close in, the whispers growing louder. Panic clawed at his chest.

And then, out of the stillness, a voice—deep, resonant, and filled with both warmth and authority—whispered in his ear:

***"Curse is a boon."***

The words echoed, lingering in the air like a chant. Kumarsen turned sharply, but no one was there. The forest remained still, as if holding its breath.

Suddenly, he felt himself falling, the ground beneath him giving way. His body jolted, and his eyes flew open.

Kumarsen sat up with a start, his breath coming in quick, shallow gasps. The clearing where he and Taran had stopped to rest was quiet, the only sound the gentle babble of the nearby stream. The stars above twinkled serenely, oblivious to the turmoil in his mind.

Taran stirred beside him, half-asleep. "What happened?" he mumbled, rubbing his eyes.

Kumarsen ran a hand through his hair, still trying to steady his racing heart. "A dream," he said, his voice barely above a whisper. "I saw Neeladri. He...he vanished, but then he spoke to me."

"What did he say?" Taran asked, now fully awake, his curiosity piqued.

Kumarsen hesitated, the weight of the words pressing heavily on him. "He said, 'Curse is a boon.'"

Taran frowned, the cryptic message sparking a flurry of questions in his mind. "What does that mean? A boon? How can a curse be a boon?"

Kumarsen shook his head. "I don't know. But it felt...real. As if Neeladri was trying to tell me something important, something we've missed."

Taran placed a reassuring hand on his shoulder. "We'll figure it out. Let's get back to the village first. Maybe the answer lies there."

Kumarsen nodded, the dream replaying in his mind like a riddle waiting to be solved. They gathered their belongings and resumed their journey, the stars guiding them home.

As they descended further, the forest seemed different—less ominous but no less mysterious. The memory of Neeladri's words lingered in Kumarsen's thoughts, intertwining with the truth revealed by the yogi. The land was cursed, yes, but perhaps its purpose was greater than anyone had understood.

For now, the answers remained elusive, but Kumarsen knew one thing for certain: the mountains held secrets that defied human understanding, and Neeladri was at the heart of it all.

The temple premises was alive with murmurs of anticipation. The cool mountain air carried the sharp scent of pine, mingling with the faint smoke rising from chimneys. Lanterns glowed softly, casting flickering shadows on the gathered villagers. Rayan stood at the center of a growing circle, trying to address the concerned crowd, but his words were drowned out by the chatter.

"They've been gone for days," an elderly woman said, her voice cracking. "If they've returned, they must have answers."

A young boy, perched on a nearby fence, added, "I heard the Nandan trek is hard. No one goes up there anymore."

"They say the yogi guards secrets that even our ancestors fear to speak," another villager whispered, clutching her shawl tightly.

As Kumarsen and Taran emerged from the misty path leading into the square, a hush fell over the crowd. The sight of them—dusty, weary, but resolute—set off a wave of murmurs.

"**They've returned!**" someone exclaimed.

"All the way from Nandan Mountain," another marveled.

Rayan stepped forward, his face betraying a mix of relief and concern. "Kumarsen, Taran," he called out, his voice carrying over the crowd. "You've been to the yogi. What did you learn?"

Kumarsen glanced at Taran, who gave him a nod of encouragement. Stepping into the center of the circle, Kumarsen raised a hand to quiet the villagers.

"I have the answers," Kumarsen said, his voice steady but grave. "But they are not what you expect. The curse… it is real. But it's not just about the land. It's about every one of you—your families, your ancestors, and the lives you've built here."

The villagers leaned in, their expressions a mix of fear and curiosity.

One man, his voice trembling, asked, "What do you mean? What did the yogi tell you?"

Kumarsen began pacing slowly, his words deliberate. "The journey to Nandan Mountain was harsh. Cold winds cut through us, the paths were treacherous, and every step felt like it could be our last. But we reached the yogi, a man who has lived on the edge of the world, guarding truths too heavy for most to bear."

"The yogi spoke of the origins of our village," Taran interjected. "Of the man who first settled here, of his struggles, and the desperate pact he made to survive."

Gasps rippled through the crowd.

Kumarsen continued, "The curse is rooted in a promise unfulfilled. The man who founded this village called upon forces he did not fully understand. In his desperation, he made a vow to a dark power—one that demanded loyalty and reverence in return for prosperity. For years, the promise held. The land flourished, and the people thrived. But the pact was broken. The dark power was betrayed, and its wrath lingered, waiting."

A woman near the front clutched her chest. "Are we being punished for something our ancestors did?"

"Not punished," Kumarsen said firmly, "Neeladri saved us". The curse is not just about the land. It is a reminder—a warning to respect the balance of the mountains, to honor the life they sustain, and to avoid greed and destruction."

Rayan stepped closer, his voice rising. "If this curse is a warning, why has Neeladri, our protector, told us to stay away from the land? Why has he not lifted the curse?"

Kumarsen met his gaze. "**Because the curse serves a purpose**. Neeladri, in his wisdom, knows that fear can preserve what greed might destroy. The cursed land is barren because it must remain untouched. It is a symbol of restraint—a lesson for us all."

The crowd began murmuring again, some nodding in agreement, others looking uneasy.

A young man called out, "But what about Asuran? He doesn't care about curses or gods. He wants to take the land and build on it. What if he succeeds?"

Kumarsen's face darkened. "If we allow greed to prevail, the curse will not remain confined to the land. It will spread, consuming everything we hold dear. The mountains themselves will turn against us."

At this, the villagers grew restless.

Another voice from the back shouted, "What do we do? How do we protect the land and ourselves?"

Kumarsen raised his hands, urging calm. "The answer lies in unity. We must stand together, as our ancestors did when they first settled here. We must honor Neeladri's wisdom and heed the warnings of the past. This is not just about a piece of land—it is about the soul of our village, our connection to the mountains, and the legacy we leave for future generations."

The village square was alive with a strange, haunting energy. The cold wind howled through the valley, carrying with it the whispers of the mountains, as though they too were waiting for what was about to unfold. It was a no-moon night, and the darkness seemed alive, pressing in on the gathered crowd. The flickering light of fire sticks cast long, eerie shadows across the stone temple and the surrounding trees.

Villagers, wrapped in heavy woolen shawls to shield themselves from the biting cold, stood huddled together. Their faces were a mix of fear, anticipation, and a desperate hunger for answers. Rayan, the priest stood near the front, his hands gripping the wooden staff that symbolized his authority. He watched Kumarsen with an expression that flickered between trust and doubt.

At the center of it all was Kumarsen, his figure towering in the wavering light. Despite the exhaustion etched on his face, there was a confidence in his stance that silenced even the faintest murmur among the villagers. By his side stood

Taran, the outsider who had become an unlikely ally in uncovering the truths buried deep within the mountains.

The wind picked up, carrying a chill that made the villagers clutch their shawls tighter. Kumarsen took a step forward, his shadow stretching across the uneven ground, and raised his hand to command silence. The crowd obeyed, their whispers dying away, leaving only the sound of the wind and the occasional crackle of fire.

"The curse," Kumarsen began, his voice steady and resonant, "is not just a tale to scare us. It has a meaning. A deep, powerful meaning that ties us all to this land, mountains and its gods."

The villagers exchanged uneasy glances. Some shuffled their feet, while others leaned in closer, eager to catch every word.

"For generations," Kumarsen continued, "we have lived in these mountains. But it wasn't always so. When our ancestors first arrived, there were no roads to guide them. No hospitals to heal them. No food to sustain them. No shelters to protect them from the merciless winters. There was nothing here but harsh, unyielding mountains."

An older man in the crowd nodded, his weathered face reflecting a lifetime spent battling the very land that gave him life.

"Our ancestors had no reason to stay," Kumarsen said, his voice growing louder. "They could have turned back, returned to the plains where life was easier. But they didn't. They stayed. And do you know why?"

The question hung in the cold night air.

A young boy whispered to his mother, "Why?" She hushed him, her eyes fixed on Kumarsen.

"They stayed," Kumarsen said, "because they had no choice. They had nowhere else to go. They were desperate—desperate for food, for shelter, for a place to call home. And so, they looked to the mountains not as a challenge to conquer, but as a hope to cling to."

A woman in the crowd spoke up, her voice trembling. "But how did they survive? How did they build a life here when there was nothing?"

Kumarsen turned to her, his expression grave. "They survived because nature allowed them to. And because the gods took pity on them. Neeladri, our protector, knew their plight. He saw their struggle and gave them permission to stay. But there was a condition."

The villagers leaned in, their breath visible in the cold night air.

"What condition?" a young man asked.

"That they live in harmony with the land," Kumarsen said. "That they take only what they need and give back whenever they can. The gods allowed our ancestors to shape the land—to carve mountains into terraces for farming, to clear forests sparingly—but always with respect and restraint. And in return, the mountains provided for them."

There was a murmur of agreement from the older villagers, but the younger ones looked uncertain.

"Those first settlers," Kumarsen said, "built a life here not because they wanted to, but because they had to. They endured the winters, the landslides, the storms—not because they were stronger than the mountains, but because they worked with them. They knew their place. They honored the gods and the land."

"But what about the curse?" Rayan asked, his voice cutting through the murmurs. "Where does it fit into this?"

Kumarsen's gaze turned to him, and for a moment, the firelight reflected a flicker of something ancient and powerful in his eyes.

"The curse," Kumarsen said, "is not a punishment. It is a reminder. A warning from Neeladri that the balance must be maintained. That we must not forget the hardships of our ancestors, nor the blessings that allowed them to survive. It is a tool to keep us on the right path."

The crowd fell silent, the weight of his words settling over them like the cold mist rolling in from the mountains.

"But look around now," Kumarsen said, his voice heavy with sorrow. "Those terraces, once bursting with life, are barren. The forests, which once echoed with the songs of birds, are being felled to make way for concrete shells that stand lifeless within a generation. Our villages, once thriving with the laughter of children and the wisdom of the old, are becoming ghostly relics of a forgotten time.

"Mountains," Kumarsen continued, his voice growing stronger. They have a limited capacity to bear the weight of civilization. Our gods understood this. Neeladri allowed the mountains to be shaped by human hands only so far as was necessary for survival. But now, we violate every sacred principle. Roads cut through the hills, scars on the face of the mountain. Rivers, the lifeblood of these lands, are imprisoned by dams. The balance is broken.

"And what of the culture, the heritage, the essence of these mountains?" Kumarsen asked, his voice rising. "It is at stake. The younger generation, seduced by the glitter of cities, leaves behind the land that bore them, abandoning the gods who protected their ancestors. They sell this sacred land to outsiders, businessmen who see the mountains not as a home, but as a commodity—a view, a resort, an investment. These mountains, the very soul of our existence, are being treated as use-and-throw material."

A whisper of agreement rippled through the crowd, the flickering firelight reflecting the despair in their eyes.

"But Neeladri knew," Kumarsen said, quieter now, yet no less resolute. "He knew that fear is the only force powerful enough to keep humanity in check. The curse—do you understand it now? It is not a punishment. It is a safeguard, a necessity. Fear is a part of us, woven into the fabric of our existence. Without it, we lose the ability to respect the boundaries that nature has set. Without it, we forget what it means to be human."

The villagers shifted uneasily, the weight of his words pressing down on them.

"Because of this fear," Kumarsen continued, "many of you, who left for the cities, still return once a year to pay homage to your gods. And that connection, fragile as it is, keeps the balance from completely unravelling. But for how long? When even that fear fades, when even that tenuous bond is severed, what will remain of these mountains?"

He paused, letting the silence stretch, the crackling fire the only sound in the heavy night air.

Taran stepped forward, his voice calm but firm. "As someone from the plains, I've seen what happens when balance is lost. Fertile lands turn to deserts. Rivers run dry. Forests vanish. If you do not protect the mountains, they will not protect you."

The crowd nodded their expressions a mix of resolve and reverence.

"But the curse," someone said.

Kumarsen turned back. "The curse is not unstoppable. "Neeladri saved our ancestors". "But will we save ourselves? Or will we allow these mountains to be destroyed by arrogance, by greed, by ignorance? The curse is not just a warning. It is a choice. A reminder that we must live with the mountains, not against them. That we must honor the gods, the land, and the balance they have tried so hard to preserve." It is a message, a plea from the gods to set things right. If we change our ways, if we honor the balance, the curse will fade.

The night air clung to the village, cold and heavy, as the flickering torches lit up the gathered crowd. Kumarsen stood before them, his voice steady but his heart pounding. He had spoken the truth, woven the pieces together, and laid them bare for all to see. Now, it was up to the villagers to decide.

A hush fell over the crowd. The whispers had started—small, cautious exchanges between neighbors, hesitant nods, and murmurs of agreement. Kumarsen stood tall, his eyes scanning the faces of the people he had known his entire life. He could see the spark of understanding growing, the way the weight of his words was sinking into their hearts.

The village square slowly came alive with the sound of conch shells and bells echoing through the cold air. It was time for the evening pooja. The villagers, still buzzing with the impact of Kumarsen's words, began to gather at the temple dedicated to Neeladri. The air was thick with the fragrance of burning incense and the soft glow of oil lamps, their flames flickering against the darkening sky.

The drums began softly, a steady rhythm that echoed through the village. Bells chimed, their clear tones piercing the dense silence. The villagers held their collective breath as Rayan raised his hands, calling for the sacred moment to begin.

As the chants started, a powerful stillness fell over the crowd. The temple idol of Neeladri, carved with precision centuries ago, seemed to shimmer faintly under the dim fire stick. Rayan, dressed in ceremonial robes, closed his eyes and recited the ancient verses, his voice steady and resonant.

Suddenly, the idol of Neeladri began to glow. At first, it was subtle—a faint aura of golden light that emanated from the figure. But within moments, it grew brighter, intensifying until the entire temple was bathed in an ethereal radiance. Gasps rippled through the crowd as the light poured out, wrapping around the villagers like a warm embrace.

A brilliant flash of light erupted, streaking from the idol straight into Rayan. He staggered for a moment, his body rigid, his eyes glowing with a celestial hue. The chanting faltered as the villagers stared in awe. Then, with an elegance that defied human limits, Rayan stood tall, his presence commanding and serene.

"**Rise, my people. I have come to meet you all.**" The voice was Rayan's, but deeper, resonating with a divine authority that sent shivers down every spine.

The villagers dropped to their knees, their fire sticks and torchs trembling in their hands. Kumarsen's throat tightened as he joined the others in silent reverence. Neeladri, the protector of their mountains, had descended among them.

The villagers brought their offerings of water, flowers, and sacred grains to the temple steps. With delicate, almost human gestures, Neeladri—through Rayan—accepted them. He lifted the humble pots of water to his lips, drinking deeply, his movements fluid and reverent. The crowd watched, their silence broken only by the crackling of the torches and the occasional sob of overwhelmed devotion.

After finishing the offerings, Neeladri stepped forward, his glowing eyes scanning the crowd. "**You have come, curious for the secret of the curse. It draws more of you today than even the annual ceremonies. Why now? Why do your hearts stir for answers that have been carried through the ages?**" His voice was calm but probing, the divine cadence striking a chord deep within every villager.

The crowd murmured hesitantly, unsure how to respond. Kumarsen, emboldened by the weight of the moment, stepped forward. "Lord Neeladri, we seek your guidance. Outsiders encroach upon our land, our traditions waver, and the mountains cry for mercy. Is the curse you proclaimed our punishment? Or is it a protection against ourselves?"

Neeladri tilted his head, the divine light from his eyes softening. "**The curse was never meant to punish. It was a warning, a barrier set to protect you from your own arrogance. This land, blessed and cursed, exists for those who respect its soul. But over time, respect has faded. Greed, abandonment, and neglect have taken its place.**"

The villagers listened intently, their faces pale in the torchlight. Some exchanged glances, guilt evident in their eyes. Others clutched their hands together, seeking reassurance from their silent prayers.

"**You wonder about the secrets of the curse, but the truth lies within your hearts. This land is bound to me, as you are bound to it. When you leave, when you allow others to desecrate what is sacred, the bond weakens. The mountains cannot bear your absence. And so, the curse remains, ensuring that no one—neither outsider nor deserter—can claim what is not theirs.**"

A brave young man from the crowd raised his voice, trembling but resolute. "Lord Neeladri, if we honor you, if we protect the mountains, will the curse be lifted?"

Neeladri's gaze turned to the man, a faint smile gracing Rayan's lips. "**The curse is not a shackle but a shield. It will lift when the balance is restored. When the mountains no longer cry for their lost children, and when those who remain honor their ancestors, then will you see the curse transform into a blessing.**"

The villagers nodded, their expressions a mixture of hope and determination. But the demigod's next words struck like thunder.

**"Beware, my people. Not all who walk these lands have your best interests at heart. There are those who see these mountains as resources to exploit. They will mask their greed with promises, but their intentions are poison. Do not falter. Stand united, or all will be lost."**

Kumarsen felt a chill run down his spine. Neeladri's words were a clear warning about Asuran and those like him. He glanced at the crowd and saw the realization dawning on their faces.

Neeladri continued, his voice softer but no less powerful. **"Do not let fear rule you. Let it guide you. Fear of losing what is precious keeps you vigilant. But fear alone cannot sustain you. Faith, unity, and action must follow. Protect the mountains, honor the bond, and I shall remain with you, as I always have."**

As the divine presence began to wane, the golden light surrounding Rayan flickered. Neeladri's final words echoed through the night, reverberating in the hearts of everyone present.

**"The mountains are alive, as am I. Protect them, and you protect yourselves. Betray them, and you betray your future. The choice is yours, my people. But know this: I will always watch over you, ready to rise when you call."**

With that, the light faded, and Rayan collapsed to his knees, gasping for breath. The villagers rushed forward, supporting him as he regained his senses. Tears streamed down his face, and his voice trembled as he spoke.

"He was here," Rayan whispered. "Neeladri was here."

The villagers, overcome with emotion, bowed their heads in silent reverence. Kumarsen looked at Taran, who stood beside him, equally awestruck.

"What now?" Taran whispered.

Kumarsen's eyes burned with determination. "We honour Neeladri's words. We protect our land. And we fight for the future of these mountains."

The crowd began to disperse, their firelights lighting the way back to their homes. The air felt lighter as if the mountains themselves had sighed in relief. But as Kumarsen turned to leave, he couldn't shake the feeling that Neeladri's warning had been more than just a prophecy—it had been a test.

And the true battle, he realized, was only beginning for the mountains and its people.

***

## Books By This Author

Title- Leo and the year 2019

Published – June, 2023

Leo and the Year '19 is a touching tale that follows the diaries of a roadside adopted dog in a sophisticated high-rise apartment building. As narrated by Leo himself, he experiences good and low points in his life as a result of not being loved by other members of society owing to his unknown pedigree. As Leo and his family encounter life's inevitable obstacles, his adorable smart canine soul provides joy, emotions, and feelings to their journey. Everything was swimmingly in Leo's life until the end of 2019, which turned the globe upside down. The story is filled with humor, tragedy, and insights that will force readers to turn the pages until they reach the last page.

www.ingramcontent.com/pod-product-compliance
Lightning Source LLC
Chambersburg PA
CBHW031522180726
48282CB00056B/203
* 9 7 8 9 3 3 4 2 4 6 3 2 2 *